He couldn't deny the exhilaration of today.

And today he didn't want to. Sarah made him feel alive. He'd take today while it was on offer and just enjoy it.

Ryan rolled on his side to look at Sarah, who lay with her eyes closed, savouring the rays of the setting sun.

Her long dark lashes curled up from her smooth cheeks and salt glistened white on her skin.

He rolled over. God, this was ridiculous. With every passing moment he wanted her more. He wanted to take her in his arms and kiss her until her eyes were wide black discs of desire, her skin was blush-pink with longing, her breath was ragged with yearning and she just melted against him, her legs weak with need.

Always an avid reader, **Fiona Lowe** decided to combine her love of romance with her interest in all things medical, so writing Medical Romance™ was an obvious choice! She lives in a seaside town in southern Australia, where she juggles writing, reading, working and raising two gorgeous sons, with the support of her own real-life hero! You can visit Fiona's website at www.fionalowe.com

Recent titles by the same author:

HER MIRACLE BABY
THE NURSE'S LONGED-FOR FAMILY
PREGNANT ON ARRIVAL

THE SURGEON'S CHOSEN WIFE

BY
FIONA LOWE

MILLS & BOON®

First published in Great Britain 2007
Harlequin Mills & Boon Limited,
Eton House, 18-24 Paradise Road, Richmond, Surrey TW9 1SR

© Fiona Lowe 2007

ISBN-13: 978 0 263 19
ISBN-10:   0 263 19

Set in Times Roman 10½ on 12¾ pt
15-0107-46448

Printed and bound in Great Britain
by Antony Rowe Ltd, Chippenham, Wiltshire

THE SURGEON'S
CHOSEN WIFE

To Mum and Dad for their constant love and support.

And to my sister, Sue, for the love and laughs and for joining me in philosophical ramblings.

CHAPTER ONE

Peace at last.

Dr Sarah Rigby pushed her arms out in front of her in a glorious cat-like stretch and spun her wrists in a circle, before leaning back onto the soft leather couch. She breathed a blissful sigh.

The unfamiliar quietness of her house enveloped her. She swung her legs up onto the three-seater couch and snuggled in. Just as she got comfortable, she spied Sam's roller blades by the door. How had he missed picking them up?

She shook her head, knowing how. He'd been too busy body-slamming his grandmother in an enthusiastic eight-year-old hug before rushing out the door, excited about his sleepover at his grandparents'.

She should get up and put them away but she was loath to move from her cosy cocoon. A healthy tiredness settled over her. It had been a busy week in Yakkaburra, pretty much the same as every other week.

Reaching over, she grabbed one of the many notepads that littered her life. Uncapping one of Sam's gel pens, which he'd 'accidentally' missed when packing up the set, she wrote in fluorescent sparkly green ink, "Monday, advertise *again* for a doctor." Tossing the pad and pen back onto the coffee-table, she lay back and gave a pragmatic sigh.

Yakkaburra wasn't Cairns or Brisbane. There were no bright city lights, no funky bars, no four-star restaurants. Even the tourist trade was slower here, the backpackers preferring Port Douglas and Mission Beach.

Attracting a doctor wasn't easy even though there was lots of medical work. The locals and the retirees from Victoria kept Sarah busier than she wanted to be.

She wanted, needed, more time with Sam. She rolled on her side and looked at her photo wall. Staring back at her were myriad family pictures and photos of Sam as a bald-headed baby, Sam, the green-eyed preschooler, proudly holding his father's hand, and Sam the red-headed schoolboy, excitement alive on his face. He was growing up so fast.

Now she was his only parent.

You were always his only parent. Some of the old tension washed through her. It always did when she thought of David.

Enough, it's your night off. Pushing all difficult thoughts about work and her life to the back of her brain, she slid the DVD of her favourite BBC costume drama into the machine. She settled in for four uninterrupted hours of losing herself in the romance of the story. Oh, the joy of not having to fight for use of the TV!

The snow on the screen was out of step with the Queensland humidity. Instead of snuggling under a rug, Sarah enjoyed the cool evening breeze caressing her warm skin as it wafted in through an open window. The cicadas' song chirruped intermittently, breaking the silence of the night.

'Aargh!'

Sarah sat bolt upright at the crashing sound and tinkling of glass that followed a man's anguished yell. Had it come from next door? Instinctively she grabbed her torch and her medical bag and walked outside.

Used to a long line of tenants moving in and out, she'd thought the neighbouring, run-down, Queenslander homestead was currently empty. Long shadows from the coconut and mango trees crisscrossed the garden, and goose-bumps rose on her skin. No lights glowed from the windows. Suddenly a mercy dash, all alone, didn't seem like such a great idea.

Get a grip, Sarah. You're a fully qualified doctor. Being rational didn't change the fact that the dark brought out the trembling child within. She dragged in a deep breath and pushed her feet forward.

A silver Mercedes convertible gleamed in the moon-light. Strange. The young itinerant fruit pickers—the ones she always seemed to end up being 'den mother' to—usually had cars barely held together with baling wire.

Apprehension shimmered along her spine. Perhaps she should have phoned Sergeant Jack before coming out here.

She reached for her mobile but her fingers only touched her belt. She straightened her shoulders. She wasn't in Sydney any more. This was small-town Yakkaburra.

She stopped at the base of the stairs, arcing her torch around the huge open space under the house, the light bouncing off the stilts. 'Hello? Is someone hurt?' Her voice sounded far more in control than her thumping heart suggested.

'Inside.' The word came out on a deep masculine groan.

She quickly jogged up the stairs. Crossing the wide veranda, she pushed open the old wooden front door that barely hung straight on its rusty hinges. Faced with a once imposing hall and rooms going off on either side, she called out again. 'Where are you?'

'Kitchen.'

She heard the pain threaded through his voice. Ignoring the cobwebs and the fact that this house in the dark looked a lot like Sam's favourite horror movie, the type she refused to watch, she marched purposefully through to the back of the house. She automatically reached for the light switch on the kitchen doorway's architrave.

'There's no point, the bulb's blown.'

She should have jumped in surprise but the deep timbre of the man's voice reverberated gently through the dark, the sound wrapping around her securely like a warm jacket on a cold night.

She took a step into the kitchen and swept the torch across the room. A rickety chair with one leg broken had collapsed on its side and a man lay sprawled on the floor with his back against the wall. He moved his hand to his eyes to shield them from the light.

'Sorry.' Sarah immediately moved the torch and crossed to his side, glass crunching under her feet. 'Where does it hurt?'

'I'm fine.' The words came out short, tense.

Sarah rocked back on her haunches. 'If you were

fine you'd be on your feet.' Common sense and caring infused her words.

He let out a ragged sigh. 'It's very kind of you to come and rescue me but I'm a doctor and the most useful thing you can do is fix the light bulb so we can both see and not injure ourselves on broken glass.' He pointed to a supermarket carrier bag on the kitchen table.

In the half-dark she couldn't see his face clearly but she recognised the natural authority in his voice. A man used to being in charge. 'Snap.'

'What?' An unravelling of his patience spun through the word.

'Snap. Kids' card game where you look for matches. I'm a doctor, too, and this time you're the patient. However, I agree, light would be good.' She stood up and handed him the torch. 'Here, you shine this so I can see what I'm doing.'

She carefully stood on another chair and stepped up onto the middle of the table. Did it just creak? She moved gingerly. 'Can you move the light over here, please?' It seemed to be hovering at hip level.

Reaching up, and more by feel than sight, she connected the bare bulb into the light socket. Cautiously stepping down, she quickly strode to the switch and turned it on.

'Eureka.' Light poured into the room.

She turned to face her patient and stopped short. In the full light she could see all of him—his long legs stretching out in front of him, his broad shoulders pushing against the wall and his polo shirt straining against his chest. A chest which showed all the signs of a man who spent a lot of time lifting weights. Her heart rate picked up, disconcerting her. She hurriedly pulled her gaze away from his sculpted body and took in his face.

Onyx eyes marred by shadows met her stare. The past rushed back so fast it took her breath away. She'd have recognised those eyes anywhere. They'd been a permanent feature of her adolescent dreams. She breathed in deeply, trying to regulate her erratic breathing, forcing herself to sound calm and in control. 'Ryan Harrison, welcome home.'

She moved forward, squatting down next to him and extended her hand. 'Sarah Rigby, Yakkaburra High School. We were in the same maths and chemistry class.' *Only the chemistry was all one-sided.*

She kept her gaze fixed firmly on his face waiting for recognition as she extended her arm. Her hand hovered in mid-air, and the moment stretched past polite and moved into uncomfortable.

His face remained blank. Her heart tore a tiny bit. What had she expected? Ryan had never noticed her in high school so why did she expect him to remember her fifteen years later?

She was just about to pull her hand back when he reached forward and gripped it firmly. Rockets of glorious sensation raced up her arm warming her. Unsettling her from top to toe.

'Sarah.' His voice moved over her utilitarian name, making it sound so sexy. 'I'm sorry I didn't recognise you.'

You've got no idea who I am, you don't remember me at all. Time vaporised.

Quiet Sarah Rigby, the girl least noticed. She swallowed against the pain of being unremarkable. She tossed her head in the age-old 'what-do-I-care?' action, forgetting she no longer had long hair that spun around her face to hide her emotions. *You're not eighteen any more. You're the doctor and you treat the patient.*

She straightened her shoulders. 'It's been a long time, Ryan. Back then my hair was a different style. It's gone through many transformations. It's been long, short, jagged and pink.'

'Pink?' One eyebrow rose in disbelief.

'Yes, even pink. It was during my "small town girls can cut it in the big city" phase.' She deliberately steered the conversation away from herself and went into doctor mode. She didn't want to recap her last fifteen years with a man who had no recollection of the previous eighteen. 'Let's take a look at you. What happened?'

He shrugged. 'I was trying to change the light bulb and I lost my balance.'

'Does your leg hurt?' She reached to examine it but he put his arm out, almost blocking her.

'My leg is fine.' The clipped words echoed around the kitchen.

Sarah frowned slightly. Fit-looking men like Ryan usually had a firm grip on the world, their feet securely planted on *terra firma*. 'Did you black out?'

'No.' The word shot out, defiant, almost aggressive.

Something didn't fit with his story but she pressed on gently. 'OK, but I'll take your BP anyway.' She reached into her bag for her sphygmomanometer, expecting him to refuse her ministrations.

Emotions warred on his face and very unexpectedly he extended his arm out toward her in an almost passive, resigned action, a slight tremor along its length. 'You won't find it low.'

She ignored the comment and wrapped the cuff around his upper arm, her fingers tingling as they grazed his smooth skin. *Stop it. He's a virtual stranger.*

She pulled her concentration back to the task and listened intently for the thub-thub of blood pulsing through the artery, matching the sound against the numbers on the dial of the BP machine. 'One-twenty over eighty. Textbook perfect. You were right.'

His mouth, which had worn a grim expression since she'd arrived, twitched into a reluctant smile. 'Glad you agree with me.'

Memories of one treasured conversation with him came flooding back. One day she'd managed to get him talking to her. She'd loved the way he'd challenged her to think logically and argue her point in the days she'd been convinced law was her calling. That one and only time she'd deliberately disagreed with his point of view solely to keep the conversation going, to extend her time in his company. Not that he would remember it.

She smiled at him, getting back on track. 'So, back to my very first question—where does it hurt and can you stand up?'

Tension moved through his body like a corkscrew. Muscles tightened from his jaw down to his feet, which seemed to rise slightly from their prone position. 'I'm not hurt, just bruised. Thanks for coming but I don't want to hold you up any longer. I'll be fine now I have light.'

Surprise and indignation surged inside her. He was dismissing her. *I don't think so, mate.* 'Tell me how you fell?'

'I'm not hurt, Sarah. You are free to go. You've done your duty of care and I won't sue you for not doing a complete check-up.' His closed expression matched the firmness of his words.

No way was the doctor in her going to walk away. Something was going on here and it niggled at her. The words 'Why are you still on the floor?' rushed to her mouth but she swallowed them as his gaze slid away and his head inclined minutely to his left.

If she hadn't been studying him so intently she would have missed the almost imperceptible movement. She followed his gaze.

The bare bulb threw a yellow light around the old kitchen with its aging stove and mantle piece with seriously faded and stained paper decorations. On the far side of the table, way out of Ryan's reach, lay a walking stick.

Suddenly the information slotted into place. 'You can't weight bear without the stick can you?'

He finally broke the long silence. 'No.'

'And in the dark you couldn't find it, which is why you're here on the floor.'

He tilted his head to the side. Eyes the colour of stormy snowclouds zeroed in on her face, seeing past it and into her soul. 'You should have gone into detective work, Dr Sarah Rigby. Please, pass me my stick.'

The slight pause before the word 'stick' spoke volumes. As a teenager he'd been fit, he'd ridden his bike everywhere. Sarah felt certain he hated that stick. Needed it yet hated it.

She picked up the walking stick. It was a utilitarian piece of polished brown wood but the gold metal handle marked it as expensive. She passed it to him and offered her arm to help him rise to his feet.

'Thanks, but I'd pull you over. If you just sweep up the glass, I can manage the rest.'

'Are you sure?' She hovered next to him.

'Please. Don't. Fuss.'

Each word peppered her like a pellet from a gun. She stood up and almost unconsciously ran her hands down her shorts as if straightening them. Fine. If he wanted to be Mr Independent, he could be. She should have known. At school he'd always separated himself from the crowd. A loner travelling to the sound of a different drum, not letting anyone get close.

'Any idea if there's a broom here?' She opened a cupboard and a mouse ran out. She stifled the scream that rose in her throat. She slammed the door shut. 'No, no broom in that one.' She strode across the room and looked behind the back door.

Grabbing the brush and pan off the rusty nail hammered crookedly into the wood, she crouched down and deftly swept up the glass, peeking up at Ryan just as she finished.

Laughter played across his usually serious face. 'You're pretty good with mice, Sarah Rigby.'

She wanted to be grumpy with him but she smiled despite herself. 'We have an understanding, rodents and I. We give each other a wide berth.'

'I'm sure if they knew you better they'd hang around.' His voice seemed to softly caress each word.

Sarah's mind went blank at the sound and she found herself swaying slightly toward him, just like she had when she'd been a teenager. *No!* She was imagining all this, wanting him to sound that way. Shock startled her into action. She stood up abruptly. She wasn't a teenager any more. She was a grown woman, a doctor and a mother. *And a widow—don't forget that bit.* Ryan Harrison had rejected her years ago. Today he couldn't even remember her. Right now he'd rejected her help.

She refused to make a fool of herself again.

Ryan watched her turn away to put the brush and pan on the table. Energy radiated off her in waves from the top of her silky chestnut bob down to her small feet shoved into bright green beach clogs. When she'd stretched up to change the light bulb the torchlight had caught her T-shirt straining against her pert breasts and the movement of the denim of her shorts sliding over her tight and curvaceous behind.

He trawled his memory but he couldn't place this petite woman. Surely he would have remembered those amazing amber eyes. Eyes that flashed with sparks of gold, seeing past his pathetic façade at being independent of her help. He needed her help but he sure as hell didn't want it.

And that had ticked her off. Along with not remembering her. He knew he'd blocked out a lot of his childhood in Yakkaburra—had he blocked her out, too? Never good enough for the locals, he'd left town the moment he'd finished school and he'd only been back once, to attend his grandmother's funeral.

He sure as hell didn't want to be here now, especially like this. Trapped by his body's failure to function properly.

Taking advantage of her having her back to him, he rolled slowly onto his side and up onto his knees. Pain seared him. Familiar pain, pain that was now part of him. Gritting his teeth, he pushed himself up onto the walking stick, the metal handle cool against his hand, and stood.

Sarah turned, emotions warring on her face. 'So

you're fine now, are you?' Her small hands hovered near her hips and then dropped to her side.

'Yes.' *Hell, he sounded like an ungrateful bastard.* But he needed her to leave. All he wanted was to fall into bed and forget. Forget the pain, forget the accident and forget he was back in Yakkaburra. Most of all he wanted to forget what his life had become.

He saw her scan the room. 'So you've got bread, milk, bed linen? The good neighbour in me can't just walk out of here without knowing stuff like that.'

'Neighbour?' He heard the confusion in his voice.

She smiled again and her face lit up, her eyes dancing flecks of brown and gold. His blood stirred for the first time in months.

'Yes, your neighbour. How else do you think I happened past? I heard your yell from my lounge room.' She tucked some hair behind her ear. 'Your grandmother used to live here, didn't she?'

He nodded. 'Yeah, so did I. She willed it to me. I'd always planned to sell it but life is busy and the agent kept renting it out so it's still mine.'

'Where have you travelled from?' Her voice had lost its initial friendliness as if she was now just playing out the role of the concerned neighbour.

'Melbourne.' He wasn't in the mood for polite conversation either.

She stared directly at him. 'Are you back here to live?'

'No.' The vehemence in his voice ricocheted around the room.

'Well, as long as you're sure.' She picked up her bag and slapped a business card on the table. 'I'll say goodnight, then.'

Contrition zipped through him. He walked over to her, hating the limp, wincing at every sound the stick made as it connected with the bare boards. 'Thanks, Sarah, I appreciate it that you came.' God, he sounded pompous.

She looked up at him, her expression a mixture of disbelief and something he couldn't quite pin down. 'Ring me if you need anything.'

He nodded and opened the back door for her.

She walked down the steps, into the night, without looking back.

A feeling of emptiness rolled over inside him. For some reason he'd expected her to wave. He softly closed the door when he saw her figure turn into her own property. *Well, you handled that well. Not.* On his way across the kitchen he righted the chair he'd fallen off when his leg had collapsed under him. He shoved it back under the table with more force than necessary.

Stomping down the hall to the only bedroom that had a bed, he threw a cotton sheet over the old mattress and sat down hard, the springs groaning under his weight. The bleakness of the house cloaked him. Hell, it was a run-down wreck of a place. But it had a roof, it was rent-free and it would have to do. He lay down, pulling his moulded pillow under his neck, one of the few possessions he'd brought from his house in Melbourne.

He closed his eyes and waited for sleep. But instead of sleep, images of smooth olive skin, large amber eyes with long black lashes and a furrowed look of concern filled his mind.

Sarah Rigby. Doctor. Neighbour. All woman.

Yakkaburra had just thrown him a curve ball.

CHAPTER TWO

RYAN woke to bright and blinding early morning sunshine streaming through the old wooden shutters, the complete opposite to his fully lined block-out curtains back home.

Yakkaburra.

The memory of the long journey north and his disastrous arrival here flooded back. The warbling of magpies competed with the kookaburras in the choral stakes, the laughter of the kookaburra seeming louder and more pointed. Six months ago he would have laughed, too, if someone had told him he'd be back in this house.

Swinging his legs over the side of the bed, he pulled on a pair of shorts and an old T-shirt. He needed to light the hot-water service. Arriving in the dark last night had been stupid. If he'd planned the trip properly he would have turned up this morning in the daylight with supplies. He'd have been organised rather than having to virtually camp the night in the house.

And you would have avoided looking like a complete idiot in front of Sarah Rigby.

But hindsight was a wonderful thing. Once he'd got

into the car two days ago he'd just driven, not wanting to stop, needing to get the inevitable over and done with. He'd delayed coming to Yakkaburra as long as he could. Now he had no choice.

He stood up and barbed pain sliced him. Facing the day head on before a shower wasn't an option. His leg responded to the heat, making it easier to move. Without it, he was stiff and all movement became jerky and unreliable.

He ran a day-plan through his head…shower, drive into town to the bakery for breakfast and then hit the supermarket for supplies. Picking up his stick and gripping it tightly, he braced himself for his first steps of the day, his left leg objecting as usual to his weight. Pain, hot and white, made him gasp and he focused on breathing in and out, trying to relax, forcing the spasm to ease.

Breathing hard, he made it to the kitchen. He immediately reached for water to wash down the painkillers he needed to control the muscle spasms, ignoring the voice in his head telling him he'd get a stomach ulcer, taking analgesics on an empty stomach. The sooner he got the water heater going the better.

He limped out the back door, seeing the garden in daylight for the first time. Old gnarled mango trees bowed over, heavy with fruit, fragrant frangipani with a myriad of perfect white and yellow flowers perfumed the air, and purple bougainvillea grew rampantly, covering anything that stood still. All of it dramatically different from the cool climes of Melbourne gardens.

For a brief moment in his memory he heard the chorus of children playing and running through the trees and cricket balls hitting the willow.

He shook his head. Where had that come from? His childhood hadn't been idyllic. The garden seemed more jungle than anything else. He added 'visit agent' to his mental list. He'd been paying for the garden to be maintained and it sure as hell didn't look like that had been happening.

He fought his way around the side of the house toward the hot-water service, removing cobwebs as he went and keeping an eye out for the poisonous red-back spider. He didn't need to add a spider bite to his medical history.

He squatted down, keeping his left leg straight and balancing by leaning his shoulder into the hot-water service. He opened the trapdoor and peered inside, trying to decipher the faded instructions on how to light the pilot. He pressed down on the red switch, anticipating the click-click sound of the flint.

Silence greeted him. Nothing happened and the flint wouldn't spark.

Damn. He looked around for something to make a taper to reach the gas flow, knowing he didn't have any paper inside. His brain kicked in and his stomach sank. Paper or not, he didn't have matches.

He pushed on his stick, stood up and walked back inside. He refused to let his mind roll back to the black marble bathroom in his townhouse in inner Melbourne, with its endless supply of hot water that a tenant was now enjoying. He picked up a saucepan, filling it with water.

He'd heat water on the stove, put a hot flannel on his leg, then shave and go into town. It was no big deal, he'd heated enough water for washes when he'd lived here as a kid.

He positioned the saucepan over the hot plate, blackened by years of use and recently years of neglect. He pushed the button in and around to turn on the stove, the automatic action sparking the realisation that the stove was gas.

No matches.

An expletive left his lips. Hell, he was stuck without matches. He spun away from the stove, frustration burning hot inside him. Sarah's business card glowed white against the scrubbed wood of the table.

Dr Sarah Rigby. GP. Yakkaburra Clinic.

You could go next door and borrow matches.

No, he wasn't going to play happy neighbours. She'd ask questions—women did that, doctors did that and he'd had his fill of his own profession. He just wanted to be on his own. No, he'd fend for himself like he'd done all his life even if he had to start a fire by rubbing two sticks together.

He picked up the card and flicked it face down as the memory of the warmth of her fingers caressing his arm the night before flooded him. He shoved the thought away. He had no intention of embarrassing himself in front of her again. Last night had been enough, sprawled out on the floor like a helpless baby. Crippled. Exposed. Half a man.

He grabbed his keys. He'd drive into town and risk the censure of the locals. He could deal with their antipathy better than a pair of sympathetic amber eyes.

His return to Yakkaburra wasn't the blaze of glory he'd always planned but the last six months had taught him planning was futile. He spun around quickly to head to the door. Cramp clenched at every muscle in his leg, sending a spasm so sharp shuddering through him that his leg collapsed under him. He slumped against the table and lowered himself onto the chair.

Anger surged at his body's unpredictability. He wanted to swipe something from the table, break something, but the house taunted him with its barrenness. He needed heat. There was no way he could manage driving into town. He closed his eyes against the pain and counted to ten.

He had no choice. It wouldn't kill him to ask Sarah Rigby for a box of matches. It would just add another dent to his pride, which had taken a severe battering in a short half-year.

Renegotiating the back steps, he muttered an oath about houses on stilts as his leg resisted the bending involved in going down stairs. He paused to pick a large ripe mango. Matches for a mango, it seemed a fair trade.

Two minutes later he stood on the front veranda of Sarah's house. Unlike his grandmother's Queenslander, Sarah's house was a lot newer and a combination of brick and timber. He rang the old ship's bell that served as the doorbell. The loud brass clang echoed around him and he hastily stilled the ringer with his hand. Thank goodness there were no neighbours on the other side of her.

A few moments passed, then he heard footsteps and the front door opened.

His fingers tightened against the mango in his hand.

Sarah stood in the doorway, her sleep-tousled chestnut hair standing up in crazy points. Soft cotton cartoon character pyjamas hugged her petite body, out-lining her round breasts and small waist.

Heat pooled deep inside him. White noise roared in his ears. How could a grown woman, a doctor, look so sexy in kid pyjamas?

He focused on a point above her head. 'Sarah.' He croaked out her name against a tight throat. 'Sorry, did I wake you?

For a moment she looked disconcerted but then she leaned casually against the doorpost, and smiled. 'No, I was lying in bed, thinking about getting up.'

'Are you sure?' His gaze seemed to be working independently of his brain, and it returned to her unhooked top button and the hint of a soft mound of skin nestled beneath.

She raised her brows. 'Do you want to come in before you pulverise that mango?'

Hell! Feeling like a kid caught in a candy store without permission, he looked her straight in the eye and shoved the mango toward her. 'I thought you might enjoy it for breakfast.'

'Thanks, that's very kind of you.' Laughter played through the words and eventually bubbled out into a full chuckle.

Time rolled back. Yakkaburra had always laughed at him, mocked him. A surge of anger shot through him. Was he out of touch with polite society? Did gestures like this usually merit laughter?

Her laughter faded and he followed her gaze and noticed for the first time her lawn dotted with orange. Jeez, he was out of touch. He'd forgotten. Mangoes and Queensland went together like meat and potatoes. Suddenly the irony of the situation hit him and he himself started to laugh, a deep, belly laugh, the sound unfamiliar to him. He realised he hadn't laughed like that in months.

'I've been down south too long. Mangoes have become a rare treat. I'd forgotten they're ubiquitous here.'

'Sorry, I shouldn't have laughed but at this time of year, after making mango chutney, mango jam and mango muffins, I'm at the point of composting a few.'

'Sacrilege.'

She grinned. 'Please, come inside.' She stepped back from the door to allow him through.

He hesitated. He didn't want to go inside. 'I don't want to take up your time. I'm just after some long matches or ordinary ones and some paper.'

She fixed him with an intense look and suddenly her mouth twitched as if she was compressing a smile.

At that moment he knew she'd remembered the previous night when he'd so brusquely rejected her offer to help with household items.

'You don't have any hot water, do you?'

He breathed out a long breath. 'Uh, no.'

Her eyes widened in disbelief. 'Don't tell me you slept in the house on that horrid old bed last night?'

'I had clean sheets.' His head shot up and he hooked his gaze with hers before he realised there was no censure on her face, just a trace of mirth.

'Well, that's something. I don't suppose you have any food either?' This time her voice sounded resigned.

Pride kicked in. 'Look, I know I'm not a great example of a Scout but as soon as you lend me some matches I will light the hot water, have a shower and head into town to fill the cupboards. Happy?'

'You better put mouse traps at the top of your list.' She pushed herself off the doorframe and gave him a wide welcoming smile. 'It's going to take your old boiler ages to heat up so come in, have a shower and some breakfast and then you can sort everything out after that.'

It was bad enough having to ask for matches, he didn't want to go inside, he was tired of needing other people to help him. 'That's very kind but really I only need—'

'Matches, I know.'

She leaned behind the door and produced a pack, laying them in his hand, her fingers touching his palm.

Shafts of sensation swept down to his toes.

'Are you certain that antique hot-water service of yours even works?'

The concern in her voice ate into his resolve. The dull ache in his leg sapped his energy. He thought about the state of the garden, the state of the house. Perhaps she had a point—there was no guarantee the damn thing would work. What was he really fighting here? 'I'd appreciate the shower but I don't want you to go to any trouble.'

She tilted her head to the side. 'Breakfast is GYO.'

'GYO?'

'Get your own—oh, and bring your own mango.' She turned and walked back into the house.

Ryan limped over the threshold, wondering what he'd just let himself in for.

Sarah heard the water stop. Ryan had finished his shower and would be out for breakfast soon. When her mother had drummed hospitality into her, had she meant inviting a childhood crush in for breakfast?

When the bell had rung, shattering her attempt at a sleep-in, she'd automatically thought it must be a patient who'd forgotten the number of her paging service. Never in her wildest dreams had she expected to see Ryan standing at her door. Especially not dressed in an old, soft T-shirt with comforting holes that clung to him like a second skin, outlining his broad and sculpted chest. Not after his curt dismissal of her the previous night.

The moment he'd asked for matches she'd had every intention of giving him a box and closing the door. Particularly after the way his gaze had swept over her pyjamas.

Heat rushed through her at the memory, mimicking the heat that had ignited every place his gaze had touched. *Pull yourself together. He was only staring because he's used to seeing women in sexy lingerie, not no-nonsense, generic cotton.*

But she had no use for silky sleepwear. It hadn't helped her marriage and now she was alone and didn't need it. Besides, cotton breathed.

Yes, she'd almost closed the door but he'd looked so battle-weary. His unusual dark eyes, which she remembered so well, were ringed with deep lines. Pain seemed etched permanently on his face.

He still had his pride though, and she saw how much it cost him to ask her for her help. And something in his eyes had tugged at her.

So what that he didn't remember her, that he'd crushed her heart when she'd been a kid? She was over all that. It was no excuse to be rude.

Besides, she was over men entirely, completely immune. This was just the action of a neighbour doing what any neighbour would do, helping out. And she was curious. Why was he back in town? And why wasn't he tucked up in the motel with cable TV and room service, instead of slumming it next door?

But whatever his situation, Ryan Harrison was a doctor and she needed a doctor. Yep, if she played her cards right she might just find out his story and get some help in return.

'That coffee smells good.' Ryan's deep voice flowed over her as smooth as warm melted chocolate.

She looked up from cutting fruit and her knife clattered onto the bench.

His black hair, even blacker now it was wet, clung close to his face, highlighting the day-old stubble on his jaw. Wanting to stare but knowing she shouldn't, she lowered her gaze, only to find board shorts that hung low on his narrow hips.

Her heart tripped. She moved her gaze again—surely there was some safe place to look. Long, strong legs came into her line of vision. Last night he'd worn long pants. Today a jagged red line ran from ankle to knee, slashing his left leg. It was one hell of a scar.

She pulled her concentration back to his comment, trying to cover the jolt of shock she'd experienced on seeing his left leg. 'It's hazelnut coffee.'

Surprised flashed across his face. 'Yakkaburra's obviously come a long way.'

Sarah placed a bowl of fruit salad on the table, next to the yoghurt, croissants and jam. 'Things change in fifteen years, but I order this in from Cairns. Would you like some?'

'That would be great, thank you.' His formal tone was at complete odds with his casual dress.

'Please, sit down.' Sarah indicated a chair opposite her. So many questions flashed through her mind but after last night she was determined to go slowly. Perhaps he would volunteer the information. *And hell might freeze over.*

A polite silence swirled around them as she plunged the coffee, poured some into a large mug and offered it to him. 'I need a cup to kick-start me in the mornings.'

'Is that your only stimulant addiction?' He smiled one of his unexpected smiles, one where all his tension fell away and a dimple appeared in his cheek.

Heat flickered inside her. *No, No, No.* 'Sadly, yes. As Yakkaburra's only doctor, even having a glass of wine gets tricky.' She passed him the fruit bowl. 'Help yourself, especially to mango.'

He grinned at her and picked up the spoon, digging it into the fruit. As he raised it over the edge of the bowl a brief tremor seemed to run up his arm.

Her doctor antennae went up.

His alert eyes, sparkling like a black opal, stared at her over the rim of his coffee-mug. 'Sole practice is hard work. Why did you choose it?'

For some reason his penetrating gaze unsettled her. 'It's more of a case of it chose me. I'd been living in Sydney and...' She didn't want to talk about David. 'Yakkaburra's a good place to raise children.'

He tilted his head slightly. 'And you have those?'

'I have Sam who's eight. He's having a sleepover at his grandparents'.' Time to shift the conversation around and take the spotlight off her. 'So, Dr Harrison—'

'It's Mr.' A muscle twitched in his jaw.

She smiled at his tone. Consultants hated being called Doctor. 'OK, *Mr* Harrison. Which branch of medicine have you specialised in?'

'General surgery, although I've got a big interest in laparoscopic surgery and trauma.'

She flicked a dollop of yoghurt into her bowl. 'You like your patients asleep, then?'

'I agree there are a few surgeons who choose surgery for limited patient contact, but I loved my intern years.' A soft, almost wistful smile stole across his face. 'I always enjoy my rounds, and hearing people's stories.'

A thrill of hope went through her that he might love the idea of general practice. 'I have days in general practice when all I do is listen.' She grinned at a wicked thought. 'I've got a couple of patients I'd love to see when they're asleep.'

He laughed and she found it hard to believe this was the same man she'd met the night before.

Her brain started ticking. Ryan being a surgeon was an added bonus. She handled small procedures in Yakkaburra and up until six months ago an anaesthetist and surgeon had come up from Innisfail on a regular circuit. But when the older surgeon had retired, the position had not been filled. Now people had to go to Cairns for major surgery. 'So, no job too big or small?'

Confusion crossed his face. 'You make me sound like a handyman, but I guess you're right. A straightforward appendectomy is small stuff compared with multi-trauma. But I pretty much enjoy everything.'

She picked out the mango from her fruit salad and moved it to the side of her plate. 'But you chose surgery over becoming a physician?'

He shrugged. 'My mentor was a surgeon. I spent a lot of time with him and I guess I fell in love with the action of Theatre.'

'Your mentor?'

He nodded. 'I won a scholarship to study medicine in Melbourne and a mentor was part of the package.'

Surprise filled her. 'Wow, Melbourne. That was a huge move, from one end of the country to the other.'

'You have to leave home some time.' His neutral expression was tinged with hardness.

'But you could have gone to Brisbane.' *And done medicine with me.*

He broke open his croissant and seemed to concentrate on putting the jam into the middle. 'I wanted a change. I'd endured eighteen years in this town, it was time to move on.'

She accepted the proffered jar of jam. 'Endured? It can't have been that bad.'

He stiffened. 'Yakkaburra embraces traditional families. Mine was hardly that and I was reminded of it every day.' He spoke quietly but each word was underscored with animosity.

Images thudded into her. Ryan, aloof from the high school pack and often absent from class, whispered rumours from teenage girls—rumours she'd always ignored—and Mrs Peterson, the town gossip, muttering about 'that family' before her mother had quickly rushed her away.

Had that been Ryan's attraction when she'd been at high school? The bad boy with a brain, the boy she found so much more interesting than the boy-next-door type? *Except now he is the boy next door.*

A need to defend her town surfaced. 'I think you'll find the town has matured a bit.'

'I'll reserve judgement on that.' He shifted in his chair. 'So tell me about your practice.'

She knew he'd deliberately changed the topic but she was OK with that as it was leading straight to where she needed the conversation to go. 'I'm flat out at this time of year with the seasonal fruit pickers being in town, on top of the normal load. Queensland health provides a practice nurse but Milly fell in love with a computer analyst from Perth and left a month ago. Right now I'm on my own and dealing with everything from haemorrhoids to haemorrhages.'

'Sounds busy.'

'It is. The hospital we knew as kids is now down-graded but we have five beds, mostly respite care, and a small staff.' She tried to keep her voice casual. 'So how long are you in Yakkaburra?'

He stirred milk into his second cup of coffee, his knuckles white against the silver of the spoon. 'I haven't decided. A few weeks, perhaps longer.'

'Working's a great way to bond with the town.'

'Who said I wanted to bond?' The words flowed out in an ominous growl.

She pressed on. 'You're planning to be here a few weeks so why not get involved? See the town through adult eyes.' She tried not to beg, tried to keep her voice neutral. 'I could really do with some help. What about doing one session a week, three hours, just to keep your hand in?'

Hardness lined his face, shadowed by something un-readable. 'No.'

The single-syllable word, tiny in its written form, blasted into her with its finality. With one word he'd rejected the town. Rejected her. She couldn't believe she'd even bothered to ask, put herself out there again to be pushed away, reliving the well-established pattern.

'Well, I'm glad you took time to consider the idea. Thank you.' She couldn't hold back the sarcasm.

A deeper shadow passed through his eyes, like a cloud blocking the sun. 'Look, Sarah, I'm sorry but I can't work here.'

'Can't or won't?' Her pierced pride didn't hold back. 'Is it the town or is general practice beneath you now you're a mighty southern surgeon?'

'No, that's not it.'

His tone, a blend of sadness and frustration, made her really look at him. He sat at her table, a qualified doctor who said he wouldn't work in her clinic. *I loved my intern year and I always enjoy my rounds, hearing people's stories.*

He was back in a town he hated and surgeons didn't usually holiday in run-down houses. None of this made sense. Holding back had got her nowhere. She bit the bullet, putting into words what had nagged at her since the night before. 'This is all to do with your leg, isn't it?'

Ryan met her golden eyes, which were flashing with a mixture of wounded pride and concern. Hell, she'd offered him a shower and breakfast and asked him *one* favour. But she had no idea what she was really asking. No idea that he couldn't reciprocate what she thought was a perfectly reasonable request.

He couldn't help her.

In the process of refusing he'd hurt and offended the only person in this town who had ever shown him any consideration. *Twice in two days. Good going, mate.*

How he wished he could remember her. He remembered plenty of girls, especially the rich and popular set who had made it obvious he'd never be good enough for them.

She deserved an explanation, she needed to hear that his 'no' wasn't personal. But telling her would be one of the hardest things he'd ever done.

He plastered a smile on his face, feeling the tension across his cheeks. 'This could take a while.'

She sat back, her arms folded against her in a protective gesture. 'I've got time.'

He marshalled his thoughts. Just tell her the facts. If you stick to the facts you'll be fine. 'When I lived here I used to escape town by riding my bike.'

She nodded. 'I remember always seeing you on your bike.'

Her comment surprised him but he kept focused. 'When I started medicine, cycling became a great stress reliever and then I pushed myself with it, enjoying a challenge.

'I've ridden around Port Phillip Bay in a day, I've done all the long-distance endurance rides, crazy stuff like six hundred kilometres in a weekend.'

He caught her uncomprehending look and grinned. 'It's addictive and I loved it. In fact, I used my bike more than my car.'

She smiled. 'With Melbourne's traffic you can probably get around a lot faster, although you have to dodge those trams.'

He gripped the edge of the table. 'Trams aren't the problem. Six months ago I came off second best with a four-wheel-drive.'

'Oh God.' She leaned forward as if she wanted to touch him, say more, but she hesitated and leaned back.

Thank you. He hated sympathy. It changed nothing. 'The vehicle clipped my bike and I spun out under the wheels, my head breaking my fall.' He heard her intake of breath.

'Do you remember any of it?'

Immediately the antiseptic smell of the hospital flooded him. Snatches of memories bombarded him. Screaming sirens, rushed footsteps, hushed tones, frantic yells, machines beeping, red-hot pain, impenetrable blackness and dazzling white light.

His heart pounded faster, and he forced his hands to stretch against his thighs. 'Some of it's clear.' The choking sensation of the endotracheal tube haunted him and his throat instinctively tightened. He dragged in a breath, willing his throat to relax.

'What were your injuries?' He heard the professional tone in her voice.

Focus on the clinical aspects. 'I had a closed brain injury, ruptured spleen, tension pneumothorax, shattered ankle, compound fracture of the left tib and fib, severe tissue damage to my left leg, fractured clavicle and severed tendons in my right hand.'

Her face drained of colour. 'I imagine listing all of that is the easy bit.'

Her words rolled through him, tearing at his flimsy attempt at detachment. His stomach clenched. Flashback images, jagged and fragmented, crowded his mind. *Just do a presentation report. Think of it as a Monday medical student round.*

He pushed on. 'The patient was immediately transferred to Theatre at St Stephen's. The leg was a grade three B fracture so treatment was external fixation with intravenous antibiotic therapy.' His chest tightened and beads of sweat formed on his hairline.

'The patient was in Intensive Care for four days until fully conscious and weaned from the respirator. The hospital stay was extended due to contracting methicillin-resistant *staphylococcus aureus* at the pinpoints of the orthopaedic fixation.'

The memory of the agonising wound care, stinging, fiery pain, screaming phlebitic veins from leaking intravenous drips, the red welts of inflammation tracking along his arms, all of it swamped him. He forced in every breath against a constricted chest, pulling at every fibre of control, his voice speeding up to finish quickly. He would *not* fall apart.

'Vancomycin was the drug of choice and the infection responded appropriately. Six weeks later rehabilitation commenced with physio and hydrotherapy with complete discharge achieved eight weeks later.'

Silence.

The pain of cramping fingers penetrated through the fog that engulfed his brain. He had no idea he'd been gripping his walking stick. He had no recollection of even picking it up.

'That's a very well-presented case, Ryan, but it's not exactly a holistic report. How is the patient doing now?' Her words came out softly, gently probing, stripping at his façade.

He pushed back his chair and lurched to his feet, anger and frustration surging. 'His leg is crap, it collapses out from under him at any given moment, the pain never leaves him and the tremors in his hand mean he can't control a scalpel.'

She stayed seated but her eyes never left his face. 'So you're on sick leave and up here as part of your recovery?'

He spun around, wanting to break the contact, hating the look of empathy in her large almond eyes, hating how she was pushing him to tell her everything.

Knowing he had to tell her everything to fully explain why he couldn't help her.

The lead weight of reality dragged at his belly. 'My position at St Stephen's has been terminated. As far as the hospital is concerned, I'm recovered, as good as I will ever be. The St Stephen's board slapped a 'no-operating' ban on me and bade me goodbye.'

'What about another position? Working elsewhere?'

He pictured the 'I'm sure there is a solution' expression on her oval face. He doggedly stared out into the Queensland sunshine. 'What, a surgical position for a surgeon whose previous employer won't give him a reference because they believe he can't operate?' Bile scalded his throat and the final threads of control slipped.

He turned back. 'Look, you can't make this better, Sarah. I can't work. I can't help you as a doctor. Place an ad.' He limped to the door. 'Thanks for breakfast.'

The security door slammed shut behind him. He didn't look back. He didn't need to. The image of her finely chiselled features was etched on his mind with indelible ink.

Sarah sat stunned and mute. Half-sentences and tangled thoughts collided in her mind. The traumatised trauma surgeon. His hatred of his damaged leg and unreliable arm cloaked him, pulling at her. She wished she could wave a magic wand and fix it.

But she couldn't. And he couldn't either, which clearly taunted him. He'd just lost a career he'd spent his adult life achieving. But why would he leave his home, his friends, his support network? Why leave Melbourne?

She reached for the coffee-plunger, squeezing the last quarter-cup from the pot, and tried to organise her thoughts. Ryan had always been a loner. He probably didn't have a support network.

But why would he choose to come to Yakkaburra, which he hated?

She started to clear the table. *My position at St Stephen's has been terminated.* She thought about the expensive car in his driveway.

Her eye caught her bank statement, her overdraft still very large three years after David's death. Still heavy with the debt of David's excessive Sydney lifestyle, the one he'd thought he'd deserved. The one that had collapsed like a house of cards on top of her because David hadn't taken out life insurance. *For Pete's sake, Sarah, you worry too much. Lighten up. I'm enjoying my money.*

The sound of her mobile phone pushed David's patronising voice out of her head. 'Dr Rigby speaking.'

As she listened to the worried woman's voice on the other end of the line she picked up her keys and her bag. 'Put ice on his ankle and I'll meet you at the clinic in five minutes.'

Justin Loddon had just got the ribbon for the first cricket injury of the season.

CHAPTER THREE

RYAN heard a wheezing noise. In the last week he was certain he'd heard and interpreted every single creak and groan this house could make, including the scratching of the mice and the possums that tangoed in work boots at three a.m.

Grabbing his stick, he walked down the hall, moving a bit easier than he had when he'd first arrived now he had a proper bed to sleep in and hot water. The wheezing came again, followed by a knock.

Front doorbell. Who would be visiting? He was fairly certain it wouldn't be Sarah after their last conversation. She'd thankfully given up doing the neighbourly thing and had got on with her life with her son and her...husband? Although she didn't wear a ring, and when he'd used her bathroom he hadn't noticed any signs of aftershave or a man's razor.

He pushed his thumb down on the old latch and pulled open the door.

A kid with spiked fiery red hair and bright emerald green eyes stood staring at Ryan's leg and walking stick. He swayed back and forth on his feet, words tumbling out of his mouth. 'Um, 'scuse me but my dog and ball are lost in your garden and Mum said I had to ask you if I can look for them so can I and I promise I won't break anything.'

Ryan's brain tried to catch up with the monologue. 'Sure, let's look for your dog, he's probably down the back. Come in.' He led the way down the hall and crossed into the kitchen.

He opened the back door. A brown and black dog with an expectant look in his smart brown kelpie eyes and a ball in his mouth trotted across the old lino floor, nails clacking, and dropped the ball between Sam's feet. 'I think your dog just found us.'

'Drover.' Sam flung his arm around the dog.

Something moved inside Ryan at the sight of a boy and his best mate. 'That's a cool name for a dog. What's your name?'

His small hand shot out. 'Sam. I live next door.'

Sarah's Sam. 'Pleased to meet you, Sam.' He encased the boy's hand, which felt so small in his own. 'I'm Ryan.'

'Why are you shaking?'

He'd forgotten the directness of children. No beating about the bush with kids. 'I had an accident, a car knocked me off my bike and now and then my arm just shakes.'

Sam's eyes went wide. 'So that's why you've got that awesome stick. You know, instead of that plain handle you should have a panther or something.'

Laughter bubbled up inside Ryan. 'I'll remember that but I'm hoping to get rid of the stick one day, not get a second one.' He filled a container with water and put it on the floor for the dog, who immediately lapped up the water nosily. Suddenly, for the first time in months, he felt like company. 'Do you want a glass of water as well?'

'Yes, please.'

Sarah's kid had impeccable manners but, then, his mother was big on hospitality. He poured two glasses of water and sat down at the table.

Sam looked at him. 'Did you spend all your money on your car and that's why you're living in this dump?'

Ryan half choked and half laughed, desperately trying not to spurt water out of his mouth and nose. 'Um, no, I have a lovely house in Melbourne.'

Sam put down his glass. 'My mum says this house has po-pote…'

'Potential?' Drover came and put his head on Ryan's lap.

Recognition zipped across Sam's face. 'Yeah, that's the word. She said someone should paint it and stuff and it would look really good.'

'Did she?' His hand reached around behind the dog's ears, and he rubbed, the fur soft against his fingers.

'Yeah, so are you going to do that 'cos I'm really good with paint and saws and stuff and I could help.' Hope filled his face.

Ryan leaned back in his chair and surveyed the dreary kitchen, the room he spent the most time in. He had no intention of doing anything to the house except selling it. It was just a place to exist while he worked out what the hell he was going to do with the rest of his life.

Maybe some fresh paint would help. It would help pass the time, make the days go faster. Sam seemed keen. *And you've had more entertainment in the last ten minutes with Sam and Drover than you've had in months.*

He continued rubbing the dog's ears. 'We'd have to decide on a colour.'

Sam sat forward. 'I like red.'

Ryan hauled himself to his feet. 'Let's go and ask your mother if you can come to the hardware store with me.'

'Cool.'

'Mum! Mum!' Sam came flying through the back door, with Drover right on his heels. The dog skidded on the slate floor as Sam came to an abrupt stop. 'Can I go into town? I've gotta choose paint and me and Ryan are—'

'Whoa.' Sarah held up her hands, laughing. 'Slow down there, mate.'

'May I come in?'

A shock of delicious sensation ran through her, tingling all the way down to her toes. She adored that wondrous feeling.

She wished it didn't happen.

Her body needed to listen to her brain. Ryan Harrison did not find her attractive. Never had. Not likely to. After her debacle with David it was probably just as well. She had no room in her life for a man.

She took in a steadying breath and looked up at him. His trade-mark shadows clung to him but his face had more colour than when she'd last seem him.

She smiled her hostess smile. 'Come in.'

He stepped inside the doorway, hesitant as if he was unsure of his welcome. A marked contrast to his previous fiercely independent, take-no-prisoners approach. 'Sam and I are embarking on a project and I was wondering if you'd allow him to come to the hardware store with me?'

Surprise rocked through her. 'A project?'

'Yeah, Mum, I told you.' Sam looked expectantly at her.

'Sam decided the house needed a touch-up, so I thought I'd start with paint.'

Sarah's head spun. 'And you're taking decorating advice from an eight-year-old?'

Ryan shrugged, the action reminiscent of the teenager she remembered. 'Why not?' The words challenged.

What was going on here? 'Painting means ladders, Ryan.'

He stiffened and his face smoothed into hard planes. 'I'm quite aware of what is involved in painting, Sarah.'

'Mum, we're going to paint his kitchen red.' Sam almost vibrated with excitement, seemingly unaware of the tension in the room.

She looked from one to the other, hardly believing what she was hearing. Ryan wanted to climb ladders with a leg that lacked muscle tissue and have a child help him. Had he gone completely insane? *A red kitchen.*

She opened her mouth to object, to be the voice of reason. To be the doctor telling the patient how he should do things, tell him he could fall from a ladder, outline the safety concerns...

He's lost his career, his life as he knew it. Perhaps he needs to do this.

Sometimes she hated it when her subconscious was right. Ryan needed to do this to prove heaven knew what to himself. And Sam was excited about the idea. But two unsupervised males in a paint shop? 'Maybe I should come along as well, for some colour advice.'

'If you like.' Ryan's eyes suddenly twinkled like sunshine through a kaleidoscope, as if he could read her like a book. 'But you're *not* going to talk us out of red.'

A flash of indignation was quickly chased away by a sensation of lightness and fun that fanned out inside her. 'I have no intention of talking you out of red.' She tossed her head. 'Red as a feature wall would be very art nouveau.'

'So that's a tin of Tuscan red, two tins of cream, four drop sheets, scrapers, roller and pan and two brushes.' The cash register pinged. 'I'll throw in the ladder rental for nix because you're a local.' Jim Rollins, the store-owner, gave Ryan a hearty smile. 'That old house of yours is a beauty. It's great to see you're back and doing it up as a tribute to your gran.'

'I'm only painting the kitchen.' Ryan reached for his wallet.

Sarah tried to keep a straight face.

Jim nodded, an understanding look on his face. 'Wise idea to start in the most lived-in areas of the house. Do try and keep the original kitchen cupboards to keep the feel of the Queenslander.'

He pulled out a photocopied document and pushed it toward Ryan. 'I'm president of the heritage commit-tee so as you move into more serious restoration I'm here to give you some guidance. Best to plan it in stages.' He sighed a blissful sigh. 'Those French doors on your veranda will come up a treat with new fanlights and fretwork, and I can get you a deal on patterned cast-glass panels.'

Sarah gave in and couldn't help smiling at Ryan's stunned look.

'Ah, thanks, Jim. That's very kind of you.' Ryan picked up a can of paint.

Jim lumbered out from behind the counter. 'I'll give you a hand with the rest of this stuff.'

Ryan's knuckles stiffened on his cane and a tremor rang through his body. His relaxed face twisted and his mouth flattened.

A twist of sorrow lanced her. He hated his leg, hated accepting help. She stepped up and smiled. 'Thanks, Jim, but between the three of us, we'll be fine.' She handed a can of paint to Sam, the bag of equipment to Ryan and carried the last two tins of paint herself.

Ryan gave a curt nod to Jim and walked out the shop, his spine rigid.

Sarah followed. Sam had already run ahead, eager to get home and start.

Ryan had opened the tiny space that counted as the boot in his convertible and loaded the paint.

'Just as well the ladder is being delivered.' Sarah kept her voice light.

Ryan took her cans of paint from her, his fingers brushing hers lightly as they wrapped around the handles. Pulsing trails of fiery heat whipped through her at his touch. She shivered.

'Are you OK?' His inky gaze intensified on her face.

'Fine, it's just a bit cool today.' She tried to cover her reaction to him.

He looked at her as if she'd lost her marbles. 'It's thirty-one degrees Celsius.'

'You've become such a southerner.' She quickly hopped into the car, breaking off the conversation, not wanting to embarrass herself any more.

Sam climbed into the back seat.

'Got your seat belt fastened, mate?' Ryan turned to check.

'Hey, you don't need to ask, Ryan. Look at the little green man on the dash.' Sam's small finger pointed to the light.

Ryan laughed. 'I had no idea that was there. I guess you're my first back-seat passenger.'

His laughter encased Sarah, its richness almost intoxicating. This man was a bag of contradictions. He lurched from completely closed off to relaxed and open. So many questions tumbled to Sarah's lips, driven by a desire to know more about him and his life in Melbourne.

Her pager beeped. Pressing the liquid display, the words 'clinic emergency' blinked at her.

'Problem?' Ryan started the car.

'Emergency call. I need to go to the clinic immediately.'

'Why not the hospital?'

'We don't have an accident and emergency department any more so people come direct to the clinic, which is in the hospital grounds.'

Ryan quickly reversed the car and drove to the other end of the main street. 'It's on Warragul Street, isn't it?' He slowed to turn right.

'Yes, you go right then left.'

Thirty seconds later he pulled up in the car park. A young man was doubled over and slumped by the clinic door. A very scared young woman sat with him.

Sarah swung the car door open. 'Sam, you can watch a DVD in the waiting room, OK?' She ran to the patient. 'I'm Sarah Rigby, the doctor. Let's get you inside so I can examine you.'

'Sarah, where are your keys?'

She turned to see Ryan standing next to her. She

tossed him her bag. 'Inside the zippered section. Sam will help you with the code for the security system.'

She turned back to her patient and the girl. 'Can you help me lift him up?'

The young woman nodded and put her arm through the young man's.

'One, two, three.' Sarah pulled him to his feet, surprised by his height. 'Now, hold onto my shoulder and your friend's...'

'Alice,' the young woman filled in the missing information. 'Alice and Jason.'

'OK, Jason, hold onto Alice and we'll help you to the treatment room.'

Jason groaned but managed to shuffle to the room and with Alice's help he got up onto the examination couch. He lay down, his face almost as pale as the white cover sheet. A moment later he struggled to sit up.

Sarah steadied him. 'Does it feel more comfortable to be upright?'

Jason nodded. 'Can't...always...get...air.' He held his right arm very close to his side with his forearm across his chest.

'Do you have asthma?'

He shook his head, looking scared. 'No...never.'

Sarah turned to grab her stethoscope and turned back to her patient to see Ryan putting an oxygen mask over Jason's face.

Sarah caught his eye and nodded her thanks, happy he'd decided to practise medicine today. Turning her focus to Jason and Alice, she started taking a history. 'Alice can you tell me what's been happening and that way Jason can get the benefit of the oxygen for a bit?'

Worry lines crossed Alice's flushed face. 'Nothing's been happening. Today's our day off and we were just sitting on the couch at home, watching the telly, when Jase got this really bad pain in his chest.' She wrung her hands. 'It freaked me out.'

Sarah nodded and turned back to Jason whose face had relaxed slightly behind the green plastic oxygen mask. 'Can you show me where the pain is?'

He spanned his hand across his chest and out toward his right shoulder. He looked about twenty so she could pretty much rule out a heart attack. Still. 'Any family history of heart problems, Jason?'

He shook his head.

'He's tachycardic.' Ryan's fingers released Jason's wrist.

The sweat on Jason's forehead fitted in with his raised heart rate. Along with the chest pain he had three classic cardiac symptoms. Sarah ran the stethoscope along her palm, warming it up. 'I'm going to listen to your chest. Try and take in some deep breaths when I ask.'

Jason bit his lip. 'I'll try.'

'If you lean forward, that will help.' Ryan spoke quietly, reassurance and calm infusing the words.

Sarah listened intently to Jason's air entry. The sound of rapid, shallow breaths whooshed through the stethoscope on his left side. She moved the silver cusp to his right side. She strained to hear.

Nothing.

She moved the stethoscope again. 'Deep breath please, Jason.'

Nothing.

She whipped her stethoscope around her neck.

'Can you take your shirt off, please? I need to look at your chest.'

Leaning on his stick, Ryan used his free arm to help Jason tug off his T-shirt.

'Thanks. I've never had a male nurse before.'

Ryan stilled, his jaw stiff, tension ripping through him.

A pang of guilt tugged at Sarah. She should have introduced Ryan but she'd been so intent on Jason it had slipped her mind. She waited for Ryan to correct their patient, fully expecting it.

Ryan passed the T-shirt to Alice. 'You hold onto that.'

Disbelief rocked her. Why hadn't he said anything? She studied his face and her questioning gaze hooked his.

Thundercloud black eyes relayed a message. *Don't go there.* He tilted his head toward Jason and raised his brows.

'Right, Jason, breathe in again for me.' Sarah infused a professional briskness into her voice to cover the moment.

Jason's chest moved in and out unevenly, one side larger than the other.

Percussing his back with her hands, she heard a hyper-resonance. 'Alice, there's a gown in that cupboard behind you. Can you help Jason get into that? I'll be back in a moment.'

'Will do.' Alice sounded grateful that there was something she could do.

Sarah pulled the screens around Jason and stepped away. 'Ryan.' Sarah hoped he heard the request in her voice.

She walked toward the desk and heard the dull thud of his cane against the linoleum tiles.

He spoke softly. 'He's tall and overly thin, tachypnoeic, with asymmetrical lung expansion.'

Sarah worried her bottom lip. 'Breath sounds are absent on his right side. I'm thinking spontaneous pneumothorax.'

'And you'd be right. Thin young men can just pop a hole in their lung. He needs a chest tube, underwater sealed drainage and a chest X-ray.'

He confirmed what she knew and she gave a prayer of thanks that Ryan was there. The tube would drain the air from the pleural space so the lung could expand again. 'Well, you're obviously meant to be here because I haven't inserted a chest tube since my residency. What size gloves are you?'

'No.'

His face remained impassive, as if he'd schooled it to be totally neutral, but she caught the shadow cross his eyes.

He was refusing her. This was crazy. He was far more capable of doing the procedure than she was. 'But—'

'No buts, Sarah. He needs a tube in his pleural space not a ruptured lung. I took the Hippocratic oath—do no harm.'

She wanted to yell, scream and throw a tantrum, tell him the slight tremor in his arm would not be a problem today, not in this situation. But she knew it wouldn't change his mind. 'Will you at least talk me through it?'

'Of course.' He sounded affronted at her inference he might not assist.

'Fine. I'll get the equipment.'

Five minutes later she infiltrated xylocaine into the area

on Jason's chest that needed numbing, making sure it went down to the pleura. 'This will take a few minutes to work. You'll feel some pushing and pulling but no pain.'

Jason nodded as if agreement would help lessen his anxiety.

She put the syringe down on the dressing trolley. 'Ryan is a doctor visiting Yakkaburra and he's going to assist me.'

Jason's eye's widened. 'Sorry, Doc, but you…made a good…nurse.'

Sarah admired Jason's courage to try and crack a joke even when he was so ill.

Ryan gave a tight smile. 'Put your right arm up over your head so you give Dr Rigby plenty of room.'

Jason did as instructed.

'Palpate the fourth or fifth intercostal space just anterior to the mid-axillary line.' Ryan sounded like he was reading from a textbook.

Sarah's fingers located the space in line with the nipple and painted the area with Betadine. 'Sorry, this is a bit cold.'

Jason just shook his head.

'Make a skin incision parallel to the upper border of the rib and incise downwards to the fascia.'

'Hell, Doc, I hope you can understand him 'cos it sounds like a foreign language.' Alice's worried voice sounded behind them.

Sarah laughed. 'He's just telling me where to make the cut so the tube can be inserted. Right now air is trapped between your ribs and your lung and it's stopping your lung from expanding.'

Ryan handed her artery forceps. 'Now, insert this

down to the pleura and into the pleural space, widening the hole by opening the forceps.'

She felt the resistance of tissue and then inserted her gloved finger into the hole created by the clamps of the forceps. She swept the pleural space to widen the area, feeling the edge of the lung. She checked again, she didn't want it to be the liver.

'Sarah, you can't hit the spleen or liver from that position.' Ryan's voice reassured her, as if he'd read her mind. 'Now, insert the tube.'

Using forceps, she advanced the tube into the pleural space and connected the tube to the underwater sealed drainage. She held her breath.

Jason breathed in and out and the water swung back and forth.

'Well done.'

Ryan's softly spoken praise relaxed her. She'd done it. Sure, Jason needed an X-ray but the swinging water level meant the tube was in the correct position and the air in his pleural space would drain away and his lung would expand again.

She started stitching the tube in place. 'Jason, we need to get you transferred to Cairns by road ambulance but in a few days you'll be back in Yakkaburra.'

'Thanks, Doctors.' Jason gave a tired smile as his breathing became easier. 'Guess it was my lucky day after all, having both of you here.' He closed his eyes, the effort of the last hour taking its toll.

'My pleasure.' She stripped off her gloves and patted his arm. She turned to thank Ryan, but he'd walked toward the door.

He paused, his hand on the door. 'I'll check on Sam.'

She watched the door swing closed behind him.

She shook her head. A talented doctor refusing to practise, it ripped her to pieces.

Her gut feeling told her that the hospital board had banned him from operating due to their own fear of litigation. Not because he wasn't capable.

Did he doubt his own ability?

She didn't know.

What she did know was that he *should* be working. Somehow she needed to convince him to return to medicine in some form. Starting in Yakkaburra was a good as place as any.

All she needed was a plan.

CHAPTER FOUR

RYAN had every window wide open, encouraging the breeze to dissipate the lingering paint fumes. Leaning on his stick, he surveyed his and Sam's handiwork. It had turned out amazingly well considering one painter had a dodgy leg and occasional hand tremors and the other had more enthusiasm than style.

Each day at four o'clock Sam's sneakers would pound up the stairs, followed by the click-clack of Drover's paws, and the quietness of his day would be delightfully broken by a boy and his dog, eager to be part of the renovation.

Ryan didn't want to admit how much he looked forward to the mid-afternoon. Time had always been something he'd never had enough of, now he had it in spades, moving slowly and giving him too much time to think.

Six months ago he'd have been in surgery mid-afternoon, halfway through a packed list of cases. Hell, he missed it. Last week, working with Sarah, had been the first time he'd been close to a patient since before his competency test. There'd been moments when it had felt so right. But then Jason had needed a procedure, a steady hand. And the nightmare had come rushing back.

The hospital board needs to be certain of your competency and at this point in time it is in doubt. Matthew Corcoran's words, now part of him, boomed in his head, taunting him, amplifying everything he had lost—his job, his house, his life as he'd known it.

'Hey, Ryan, what do you think?' Sam's excited voice sounded behind him.

Ryan turned as Sam knelt on the tablecloth, which Ryan had spread out on the floor. He carefully floated a large white magnolia flower in a bowl of water and the pungent perfume overrode the paint fumes. 'Mum goes mad over flowers.' Sam shrugged his shoulders. 'Girls.'

Ryan laughed. 'I think that's the finishing touch to our celebratory picnic.' He put his hand on Drover's collar. 'Sit, boy, we don't need you undoing all our hard work.'

'I can't wait to show Mum.' Sam hopped from one foot to the other, his excitement spilling over.

'I think we're ready. Go get your mum.' A crazy spurt of anticipation snuck under his guard. His time in Yakkaburra was temporary. Very temporary.

Sam whooped and raced down the back stairs.

Sam, who'd banned Sarah from visiting the house until now, wanted to show her the completed job. Ryan had been secretly relieved about the ban because he was still reeling from the previous Saturday.

From an early age he'd learned to depend on himself. People let you down. *Except for Gran.* Women had always wanted more than he had been prepared to offer. Yet, as he'd painted, his thoughts had frequently turned to Sarah, her wide smile, her sparkling eyes and the way she wrinkled her nose when she was deep in thought.

Never before had he been so distracted by a woman.

When he'd stood close to her, talking her through the insertion of the chest tube, the floral scent of her perfume had affected his concentration to the point that he'd barked out instructions.

She drew him like no other woman and that scared him. He'd never needed anyone. Work had filled his life. Now he had nothing to offer a woman. Perhaps if he'd met her before the accident, things would have been different.

But now…hell, he didn't even know what he was doing with his life, let alone involving anyone else.

Now Sarah was about to arrive and spend the evening with him. Sam had asked, begged and pleaded to have a celebration and he'd worked so hard Ryan could hardly refuse. All he had to do was be the host and share a meal. Sam would be there the whole time and he would make the perfect distraction.

'Hi,' Sarah's cheery voice floated across the kitchen. Clutching a bottle of wine, she stopped in the doorway, with Sam and Drover prancing around her legs in excitement.

'Wow! It looks so fresh and clean and welcoming.' She put the bottle on the bench and gave Sam a huge hug and a kiss. 'What a great job you've done.'

A streak of longing travelled through Ryan. What would Sarah's arms feel like around him? *That isn't going to happen.*

Sam struggled out of his mother's embrace, eager to show her the new linings inside the cupboards. 'And Ryan shoved steel wool inside all the gaps so no mice can get in.'

For the first time since her arrival Sarah looked

straight at Ryan. Her golden eyes danced with merriment and admiration. 'What a shame—a rodent-free zone.' Her face immediately became more serious. 'You've done a sensational job.'

'Thanks.' His body buzzed with her praise, which was a crazy reaction. He used to save lives. Saving lives was worthy of praise, not painting.

Confusion swirled in his gut. He wasn't used to this. Wasn't used to his body going into overdrive around a woman.

Just be the host. He opened the fridge and pulled out a bottle of sparking wine. 'Sam, you open the chips and put them with the picnic.'

He turned toward Sarah, trying not to notice how her summer tan complemented the bright pink sleeveless top she wore. But he lost the battle completely when he saw the small pendant nestled in the dip between her breasts. Heat slammed through him. Clearing his suddenly tight throat, he asked, 'Are you all right sitting on the cushions or do you want a packing box?'

She laughed. 'My hips might just be able to handle the cushions, but what about—?' She paused abruptly, as if swallowing her words. 'Where's the table and the chairs?'

He handed her a picnic champagne flute. 'The chairs are being made sturdier and the table is in the room that might one day be called the lounge. I've been sanding it down and had hoped to get it finished, but time got away from me.'

She raised her brows. 'You have been busy.'

He tried not to snort. He wasn't busy, he was killing time. 'I suppose you could say I have.'

'But it's different "busy", isn't it?' Her sincere look lanced him. He didn't want her sympathy.

The cold, hard bitterness that had entered him after the accident expanded inside him, the very same feeling that had made him so rude to Sarah when he'd first met her. A retort rose to his lips.

No! She doesn't deserve your bile. She'd never shown pity, just a piercing understanding.

'I'm starving.' Sam hungrily eyed the chicken.

'Right, let's eat.' Ryan could have hugged him for his timing in changing the topic, breaking a difficult moment.

After filling Sam's glass with lemonade, he lifted his own. 'To a job well done. Thanks for your help.'

Sam beamed.

Sarah toasted them both and then gave a self-conscious laugh. 'I confess to having doubts about this project and I'm thrilled you both proved me wrong. It's turned out great.'

They hungrily dug into the food, interspersed with a 'joke-off', which Sam won hands down. He had an inexhaustible supply.

Sarah put her plate down on the cloth and leaned back, her pink tongue languidly licking her lips.

Colours exploded in Ryan's head. He gulped down the last of his drink and refilled his glass, knowing this time the tremble in his hand had nothing to do with his injury.

'That was a fabulous meal. My compliments to the cook.' Sarah gave him her high-wattage smile.

He could sink into that smile any day. 'I'll pass them on next time I'm in the Yakkaburra Gourmet Deli.' He laughed. 'Cooking isn't one of my strong points, I never really had the time.'

'Hey, if you had made me a sandwich I would have enjoyed it. My nana used to say, "You can feed them grass and they wouldn't care."' Her tinkling laugh wafted around her. 'And she was right. If I don't have to prepare it then it always tastes better.'

'Well, we can test that theory on the chocolate cake Sam and I made.' Contentment filled him at the easy atmosphere of the evening, the enjoyable conversation and the feeling of friendship. Ryan eased his weight off the packing case onto his leg.

There was a pounding on the back door. Sam jumped up. He ran to the door with Drover fast on his heels.

Sarah stood up looking flustered. 'I'm really sorry, Ryan, but when your invitation came we'd already arranged for Sam to spend the night with my parents. He and Dad are off fishing early in the morning.' She brushed her hands down the front of her shorts in the same almost nervous action she'd used the first time he'd met her.

Disappointment rammed into him. She was leaving. Sam was leaving. Suddenly, Saturday night stretched out in front of him like a black hole. He'd been alone all week, apart from Sam's company. He craved some adult conversation.

'Can you see Sam off and stay for coffee and cake?' The words came out before his brain had censored them. This was Sarah. The woman he should not be alone with. The woman with smooth olive skin that begged to be stroked, with bee-stung lips that screamed to be kissed and thick, lustrous hair he wanted to bury his face in and breathe in her scent.

She hesitated for a moment and then seemed to shrug away whatever thought had crossed her mind. 'I guess

I could stay. I've only got an empty house to go home to. As long as you're sure I'm not holding you up?'

As long as you're sure. Hell, he wasn't sure about anything except for the first time in a long time he didn't want to be alone.

The house seemed eerily quiet without Sam's chatter. Sarah sat on an old couch in what would have been the dining room. She should have left with Sam. He had been their buffer. Now she and Ryan had lost the companionable feel they'd had when Sam had been with them. She was back to feeling like she'd always felt around Ryan. Gauche, plain and unremarkable.

Ryan shifted on the couch, moving into a more comfortable position, his leg brushing against hers. Electric-charged delight moved through her, lighting up areas that had been dormant for years. Stunning her with their intensity.

Flustered, she said the first thing that came into her head. 'You've brought the kitchen back to life, painting it with those colours. I always think kitchens are the life-blood of a house.'

'Really? I have a kitchen in Melbourne that I've spent very little time in. In fact, I followed the new trend and I didn't install a conventional oven.'

The thought of a kitchen without an oven horrified her. 'Now, that's sad.'

'No, it's practical.' A fizz of indignation clung to the words.

Her skin prickled. 'It sounds soulless. I bet it's one of those stainless-steel kitchens that are in all those decorating magazines. The ones that look more like an operating theatre.' *Just like David wanted.* The thought infuriated her. Her belly tightened.

'Here your kitchen has soul. It has a history of conversations, Sunday roasts and family decisions. What about your poor house in Melbourne? It deserves more than a sterile life.'

He looked taken aback. 'My townhouse has a view to die for, every mod con and a sound system the envy of every hi-fi aficionado.'

'Sounds expensive.' She heard the curtness in her voice, hating David's legacy on her life.

His brow creased. 'Of course it's expensive.'

His matter-of-fact tone could have been David's. *For God's sake, Sarah, anything less than six bedrooms and we'll look ridiculous. This is show business. To be successful I have to look successful.* 'Oh, so expense and the price was your guide to buying was it? Forget character, forget comfort—in fact, don't even call it a home.'

Her voice had started to rise and she couldn't stop herself. 'Just as long as it has almost four zeros on the end of the price tag and it's a house worthy of a surgeon.'

His face tightened. 'I worked damn hard for my home.' He swept his arm around the room. 'I came from not much and I started out with nothing.' A muscle twitched in his jaw. 'This accident has taken away my career—it damn well isn't going to take my house.'

The stark reality of his words hit her in the chest. Right at that moment she knew the reason he was in Yakkaburra. Her hand flew to her mouth, regret pouring through her. 'Oh, God, I'm sorry. I had no right to say what I did. Of course you have a home you love and don't want to lose.' She pressed her hands together. 'Coming back here is part of a plan to save it, isn't it?'

He nodded, the planes of his face stark and hard. 'Yes. Insurance money only goes so far.'

Her heart tore a little. His life had been completely turned upside down, everything he knew and depended on ripped away. 'So, really, the accident has been a double indignity in your eyes? Forcing you back here, a place you hated?'

He sighed. 'It wasn't quite the way I planned to come back.'

'Why do you hate the town, Ryan?' The words rushed out, releasing her curiosity.

Starless black eyes narrowed slightly and his jaw tightened. A long silence hung between them before he finally spoke, almost forcing the words out. 'The Harrisons were never quite good enough for Yakkaburra.' He breathed in deeply, as if carefully formulating his next sentence. 'I spent my childhood being told I was fatherless scum, that I would come to nothing, like my mother.' His fingers curled into a fist. 'I planned to prove them wrong.'

She spoke softly, treading carefully, handling the information like crystal. 'And you did.'

'Oh, yeah, right.' His scathing look pierced her. 'I'm back here, unemployed, half-crippled and financially strapped. Yeah, that'll really show them.'

Anger at his self-pity boiled. 'Ryan, you're a successful surgeon with a healing arm and leg.'

'I was a surgeon.' His bitterness trailed through his voice.

Everything inside her railed against his words. 'So

prove them wrong. Only this time *they* are the hospital board, not the town.'

The shadows in his eyes darkened and he pushed his right hand out in front of him, toward her. 'It shakes, Sarah. My leg collapses. Accept it.'

Her frustration and concern for him collided inside her. 'No, I won't accept it.'

'Oh, so now a country GP knows better than the top medical specialists in the nation?'

His sarcasm ripped through her but she ignored it. 'I know that you probably tried to go back to work too soon and you failed their competency test. That doesn't mean you're not going to be competent in the future.'

Scepticism pulled at the corner of his mouth.

She dragged him to his feet, almost pulling him back to the kitchen. 'Look.' She pointed with her free hand to the fine bands of colour on the wide Victorian cornices. 'A man with major tremors couldn't have painted that.'

Silence surrounded them. His hand lay hot and heavy in hers, his fingers slowly tightening against her skin.

Finally, he spoke so softly that she needed to step in closer to hear him. 'But a cornice isn't a person. When I stuffed it up, I just painted it again. I did it eight times, Sarah. Eight bloody times.'

His despair swirled into her, tinged with his heat. Heat and fear. For the first time she heard fear in the timbre of his voice, felt it in the grip of his hand and experienced it pummelling her in the chest.

She couldn't allow him to let that fear become part of him. Wouldn't let him give in to someone else's agenda, a hasty decision by a medical board driven by fear of litigation.

'Ryan, I know you want your old life back but you don't go from the bottom of the mountain to the top in one step. It has to be small steps.'

He moved slightly as if he would walk away.

She needed to get his attention, needed him to really hear her. She dropped his hand and raised both her hands to his cheeks, gently pulling his face toward her, the stubble of his five o'clock shadow gently grazing her fingers.

Tilting her head up to look at him, she locked her gaze with his. 'Ryan, you can do this, one step at a time.'

Shock and surprise flashed through his eyes, followed by something else she couldn't place. The moment, which had started out as caring and comfort, spun out between them, evolving, changing, becoming something more.

Time slowed down. He swayed toward her as if in slow motion, his forehead coming to rest gently on hers.

She could hear his breath, feel the gentle whoosh of air on her face. Her heart pounded erratically.

'Why do you believe in me?' The almost whispered words, tinged with wonder, vibrated against her cheek.

A schism of pain radiated through her. 'Why wouldn't I?'

The fingers of his left hand traced her cheek, tentative at first, their pressure slowly increasing.

Blood roared in her ears. She shut down her mind, didn't question the action, just gave herself up to his glorious stroking.

Mini-explosions fired along his line of touch, the pads of his fingers sending waves of wondrous sensation deep inside her. Wave upon wave, building in intensity, banking heat.

Her own fingers gave in to their aching need and explored his face—his high cheekbones, the lines of pain etched around his eyes, the place where the rare dimple appeared when he truly smiled. With each caress the fire inside her was stoked and her body screamed, needing to touch more of him.

Little by little the distance between them closed. His leg grazed hers, her shoulder brushed his arm, his hip met hers and his eyelashes fluttered against her skin, the feather-like sensation driving her into sensory overload.

Her tongue darted out, wanting to taste him, needing to trace the lips she'd longed to feel for so long. He tasted of wine, summer heat and simmering restraint.

In a reckless movement she flicked the tip of her tongue between his lips.

He moaned, the sound almost lost against her mouth. Opening up to her, he captured her tongue with his, filling her with heat, raging desire and desperate, hollow need that ached to be satiated.

Sweet rivers of longing melded with torrents of desire, making her legs tremble. Nothing existed except the pressure of his mouth on hers.

His need.

Her need.

Ragged longing.

Suddenly, he sagged heavily against her, the fall of his cane loud on the floor.

She braced herself to steady him but staggered slightly against his weight.

He threw himself against the kitchen bench, all contact broken.

Humid night air, thick and muggy, stole in, touching her in all the places vacated by his dry, radiating heat.

No! Her body screamed its disappointment as the throb of unfulfilled desire dragged in her belly. Her brain struggled, trying to think through the fog of lust.

Pain and anger wrapped up in utter frustration slashed his face. 'Hell, you want me to go back to work and I can't even kiss a woman any more without collapsing.'

He ran his hand through his hair, the action tearing at her. She wanted to hand him his stick, she wanted to wrap her arms around him, hold him close and tell him it would be all right.

But he'd hate her for that.

She dug deep, plastered a smile on her face and looked straight at him. 'You're just out of practice.' She took two steps and kissed him perfunctorily on the cheek, as if kissing a distant relative. She tossed her head. 'I'll help you practise any time, just let me know.'

Somehow her legs carried her to the door and out into the night.

Stunned, Ryan slid down the bench and sat on the floor. *Practise?* Did she mean kissing? He ran his tongue across his lips, savouring the remaining taste of Sarah's soft feminine scent, remembering her warm, yielding mouth, the push of her breasts against his chest, the feel of her in his arms. His groin tightened. She'd felt so good to hold, filling his arms, her heart pounding against his, affirming life.

And then his damn leg had given out and he'd almost flattened her.

He'd seen her wide-eyed look, her flushed face, her

bruised lips and stunned expression. What had he been thinking, kissing her?

He hadn't been thinking at all. He'd stopped thinking the moment her hands had touched his face, the second her earnest voice had entreated and the instant her sparkling eyes with their golden flecks had captured his gaze.

From that moment he'd lost himself in her gentle touch, in her spicy scent, in the way her curves fitted against him, her tantalising murmurings of sweet sighs and her intoxicating taste that made her Sarah. The kiss had fired his blood, aroused him to the point of pleasurable pain and had stirred the hint of a vague memory that he had no clue about.

How had he lived in Yakkaburra for eighteen years and not noticed Sarah Rigby? He made a mental note to call by the school and look in the photo archives.

He stretched out his right leg and flicked his cane over to him. *Ryan, you can do this, one step at a time.*

His brain cleared, the clarity painful as the realisation hit him. When she'd said, "I'll help you practise any time," she'd been talking about medical practice.

He'd behaved like a randy teenager. He'd totally misinterpreted her care and concern for something else. And he'd kissed her as if he had been a drowning man and she had been his lifeline. *Stupid, he'd been incredibly stupid.*

He looked up at the fine lines of paint on the cornices. Since the board had rejected him for work at St Stephen's he'd been on the run from his life. He thought about his comfortable couch at home, his telescope for identifying the ships that cruised up the bay, the plush carpet that absorbed all sound. His sanctuary. How he missed it.

He wanted it all back, everything he'd worked for. He wanted to be a surgeon. He wanted the prestige, the position, the feelings of worth the job gave him. Hell, the money would be good, too.

Small steps.

Facing patients.

The thought terrified him. Admitting it to Sarah had been the hardest thing he'd done since his failed competency test.

What if he took small steps and failed?

Failing in Yakkaburra wasn't an option.

Yeah, and existing in Yakkaburra isn't much fun either.

Tension spiralled inside him and his muscles contracted. Painful spasms whipped him. The top specialists in the country had no faith in him. Why should he believe Sarah?

He swallowed two painkillers, pushing them down his throat with water, needing the relief they offered.

You need to believe her.

He slammed the voice out of his head. He didn't need false hope. Painting and patients—Sarah was crazy to compare them. There was no connection whatsoever. But painting and power tools. Now, he could see *that* connection.

Decision made, he hauled himself to his feet and went to bed.

CHAPTER FIVE

ON WEDNESDAY at 4:15 p.m., Sarah opened her office window, leaned out and screamed. It was a glorious, cathartic scream that sent the cockatoos flying up out of the tree for a moment before they settled back down, their golden crests fluttering in the sunlight.

She waved self-consciously to Meredith Turpin, the town's postmistress, who happened to be walking past just at the wrong moment. Word would be out in a flash that the doctor was going mad.

And she was mad, spitting mad.

After their conversation on Saturday night she'd expected Ryan to take the first step to reclaiming his life. She'd thought he would come to the clinic or drop in and see her and arrange a time to do a session at the practice. Start small, gain confidence.

But she hadn't seen or heard from him. Well, that wasn't technically correct. She'd actually heard him day and night—the whirr of the circular saw, the pop of the nail gun, the grind of the sander—a cacophony of power-tool noise wafting over her fence. Big boys' toys. Tools that made Sam's eyes almost pop out of his head. Tools Ryan was hiding behind.

She understood his fear but she'd really thought she'd got through to him, convinced him to make a start at returning to medicine.

But she'd been wrong.

The only thing that had happened had been she'd made a complete fool of herself. Again.

Fifteen years ago she'd kissed Ryan Harrison. Her cheeks burned with embarrassment, not tempered at all by the intervening years. She vividly remembered the night they'd been set up to entertain a group of immature kids who'd thought themselves the toast of the town. Anyone out of the clique had existed purely for their enjoyment.

The end of year twelve party had been a boozy affair, a night of celebration and craziness, a release from the grind of exams and the fear of the future. Quiet and out of her depth, not wanting to seem like a spoilsport, she'd found herself surrounded and blindfolded by a group of tipsy girls and pushed forward into the arms of a boy.

The moment her fingers had touched the leather of his jacket she'd known she touched Ryan. That jacket had been his signature.

His lips had come down on hers like a dance of feather-soft strokes and she'd leaned into the kiss, responding to his coaxing mouth, oblivious to the hoots of the crowd.

Amazed and thrilled that he'd wanted to kiss her.

And then her blindfold had been whipped off and she'd seen the bandana across Ryan's eyes. He'd removed it seconds later.

The expression of shocked horror on his face had scorched her.

The crowd had erupted around them in howls of

derision. Julie Lamond, Miss Popularity, had doubled over with laughter and taunted Ryan, 'As if I'd kiss you.'

Sarah had run from the party, mortified. He'd thought he'd been kissing Julie Lamond. He'd wanted to kiss Julie Lamond. He had *not* wanted to kiss Sarah Rigby.

That night had been the last time she'd seen Ryan until three weeks ago.

Then three nights ago she'd foolishly kissed him again.

She hadn't seen him since. But he'd rarely left her thoughts.

She sighed, wondering what to do next. She could be neanderthal woman and go and drag him by the scruff of the neck into the clinic. Her lips twitched at the image. Fun, but not remotely practical.

Meanwhile, she was here and he was at his house, spending more time with Sam than she was. A jagged pain edged in around her heart. Sam attached himself to men—her father and now Ryan. He so desperately wanted a dad.

But she couldn't face another marriage.

In his offhand way, Ryan had involved Sam in his renovation project, allowing the boy a chance to be a small man, not molly coddling him like she did. She appreciated that and the experiences Ryan was giving Sam.

But he was driving her crazy on two fronts.

The man had spent the week replacing the veranda rails, cutting and jig-sawing the new fretwork with such fine precision that she couldn't help but be impressed. As each day passed, the former glory of the old Queenslander started to shine under his skill. It was ludicrous to think he could be unsafe around patients. He'd be more than safe—he'd be an asset.

He just had to see it himself.

'Sarah!' Jenny, her receptionist-cum-nurse, sounded frantic. 'Jim Rollins has collapsed at the hardware store.'

She grabbed her keys and medical bag and ran down to Reception. 'I'm on my way. Apologise to my next few patients, please. I can see them later tonight or, better yet, squeeze them in tomorrow.'

Jenny nodded, already picking up the phone. 'Will do. You go.'

Two minutes later Sarah pushed open the glass doors of the familiar shop, the scent of freshly cut wood assailing her nostrils.

Ron McKinney, self-appointed guide, directed her. 'He's out the back, Doc, and—'

She nodded, not pausing, and ran down the central aisle, not really hearing the last bit of his sentence.

She rounded the cashier's counter, her eyes scanning the warehouse behind the shop front.

'Over here.' Ryan's deep, commanding voice made her turn.

A spark of desire flared and faded. Even in an emergency the timbre of his voice affected her and she hated that. Hated that her body overruled her head.

Jim lay crumpled on the cold, hard, concrete floor, his face ashen, his right arm hanging floppily by his side.

A jet of fear surged through her for her friend. She pushed her feelings aside the way every country doctor has to, compartmentalising her emotions.

Ryan knelt awkwardly next to Jim, having pulled him into the lateral coma position to keep his airway clear. His hand gripped a small torch.

'Thank goodness you're here.' She dropped to her

knees next to Ryan, his presence trickling some relief over her desperate concern for Jim. 'What happened?'

Ryan rubbed the back of his neck. 'I don't know.' His voice had a slight vibrato sound. 'I came in to get more wood and to check with Jim on the external heritage paint colours. The shop was quieter than usual so I came looking for him. I found him like this. I've called an ambulance.'

Sarah took out her stethoscope and portable BP cuff. As she wrapped the cuff around Jim's large arm, she listened intently to Ryan.

'Using the Glasgow coma scale, he's not looking good.' His voice steadied. 'He has no verbal response, his motor response is poor, he seems to have a right hemiparesis and his pupils are unequal in size and react sluggishly to light.' The words came out crisp, precise and professional. But his drawn expression betrayed his personal concern for Jim.

She pulled the stethoscope out of her ears, thankful she had another doctor with whom to talk through the symptoms. 'His BP's really high and his pulse slow. Any sign of injury?'

Ryan nodded. 'His temple connected with the floor but I've got a strong feeling he might have had a bleed before he fell.'

'Stroke?' She rubbed her eyes. 'Last time I saw him his BP was fine.'

Ron McKinney stuck his head through the door, his face pale. 'Will he be OK?'

Ryan turned toward the builder. 'That's what we're trying to find out, Ron. You're here most days. Has Jim complained of feeling unwell?'

'Just the usual allergy headache from the kapok.'

Sarah caught Ryan's look, sharing a moment of synergy, being at one with a thought and diagnosis. Jim was bleeding into his brain.

'Did he ever mention what sort of headache it was—dull, intense, sharp?' The urgency in Ryan's voice was unmistakable.

Ron flinched. 'Gee, Doc, I don't really know except he'd been complaining of it for the whole week. I'm just pleased you found him and that you're a medic.' He scratched his head. 'You surprised us all with that bit of info.'

'Thanks, Ron.' Sarah filled in for Ryan who had turned back to his patient, checking Jim's pupils again.

'Any change?' Sarah hoped against hope for a positive answer.

Ryan shook his head. 'He's getting worse.'

Sarah's mobile rang, the incessant ring adding to the tension. She checked the caller and flicked the phone onto speaker. 'You better listen to this, I doubt it's good news.'

'Dr Rigby, Helen Finnegan.' The ambulance dispatcher's voice came down the line. 'We have a problem. There's been a motor vehicle accident on the Yakkaburra-Cairns Road. Two ambulances are attending and as you are in attendance with your patient we have had to move you to priority two. We have dispatched a third road ambulance but it's more than an hour away.'

Sarah groaned. 'What about the helicopter?'

'It's airlifted a critical patient from the MVA and will be sent to you as soon as it's free, if you require it.' The professional voice paused for a moment. 'I'm really sorry, Sarah. How's Jim?' The conflict in Helen's voice travelled down the line.

'We need the chopper—send it as soon as you can.' Sarah jabbed the off button on her phone, her frustration focused on the tiny red button.

'This is insane.' Ryan's voice rose. 'The man needs to be in hospital.'

Sarah shrugged. 'This is the country and resources are limited. We have no choice but to deal with it.' She re-checked Jim's condition, using the GCS, hoping for a sign of slight improvement, an upward swing in the numbers.

Ryan's hand touched her shoulder, a mix of reassurance and reality. 'Sarah, you can keep doing that but he's bleeding into his extradural space.'

For a brief moment she dropped her head in her hands, hating that Jim was in this position, hating that they were all in this position. She forced herself to look directly into his ink-black eyes, knowing what he would say but needing to hear it anyway. 'And the pressure needs to be released.'

He nodded. 'He needs burr-holes.' His grim expression said it all. 'And we have to do it.'

'But we're a country hospital. Hell, we only have the basic equipment for minor procedures. The theatre's hardly used.' Panic started to build. 'He needs to be in Cairns, in ICU, with a neurologist.'

Ryan's hand lingered on her shoulder, radiating control and calmness, the complete opposite of how she felt. She was a GP, she didn't do emergency brain surgery. She wanted to absorb his composure, use it to focus her spinning thoughts.

Ryan squeezed her shoulder and removed his hand.

'This is the country, resources are limited and we have no choice but to deal with it.'

Her own words slugged her. 'But we don't even have an ambulance to transport him to the hospital.'

'We use Ron's ute.'

Ryan made it sound all so easy. Her brain raced, trying to keep up. 'Have you done burr-holes before without neurological support?'

'Yes.'

The word rang clear, free of doubt. The surgeon was back.

He fired into action. 'Ring your hospital staff. Tell them to set up Theatre and lay out every set of forceps they have. Get them to double-check the oxygen and suction and have the steriliser on standby, ready for use.' He called out to Ron who'd left the room. 'Ron, how well do you know the layout of the shop?'

'Pretty good—why?' The builder gripped the architrave.

'I'm going to need a brace and bit, with the finest drill size you have. Smaller than three-sixteenths.'

Ron's eyes widened and his face sagged in shock. 'Don't you think your shopping can wait until after the ambulance has come?'

Ryan's expression stayed neutral but his voice softened slightly. 'Ron, Sarah and I need to operate on Jim—we can't wait for the ambulance. We have to open up the old operating theatre at Yakkaburra and transport him there in your ute.'

Sarah filled in the gaps. 'We think Jim has bled into the space between his skull and his brain. The blood is pressing on his brain and if we don't release the pressure he could die.' She tried to reassure him. 'If he was in Cairns hospital we'd be using the same equipment, an old-fashioned bit and brace.'

Ron stood a bit taller. 'Right, then, I'll go and get it.'

Ryan quickly primed an IV line, swabbed Jim's arm with sterilising alcohol and handed the wide-bore cannula to Sarah. 'Insert that, and we'll establish a line with saline. He needs mannitol to bring down the swelling, which I'll put up at the hospital.' He lurched to his feet. 'I'll get Ron to bring the ute around to the warehouse doors.' He quickly limped away.

Sarah located a vein, and muttered thanks for small gifts. Jim needed all the breaks he could get. As the needle slid into place, realisation thundered into her.

Ryan was running the emergency, calling the shots, organising everyone, including her, but he'd effectively avoided inserting the IV himself. Had avoided anything that needed a steady hand. She taped the IV in place. Surely he would do the burr-holes? A niggle of concern suddenly expanded inside her, forcing the air out of her lungs. He *had* to do the burr-holes—surely there was no choice?

Ten minutes later they transferred Jim into the old operating theatre at the downgraded Yakkaburra hospital. Ryan had a sensation of stepping back in time about twenty years when he saw the set-up. St Stephen's had retired theatres like these before he'd started medicine.

An anxious woman met them at the theatre door. 'I've set up as instructed and I've called Karen in so she can be scout nurse.'

'Excellent. Thanks.' Sarah gave the woman's arm a brief squeeze. 'Jenny, this is Ryan Harrison, a general surgeon from Melbourne, although he grew up here.' Sarah briefly introduced them before doing a set of observations on Jim.

Surprise chased some of the worry from the nurse's face. 'Thank goodness you're home. How's Jim?'

Home! Not likely. 'He needs to be tubed.' Ryan heard his curt tone and silently swore. Yakkaburra sure as hell wasn't home. He couldn't do 'nice' right now, not while Jim's life hung in the balance. What if *he* made it worse? Damn it, Yakkaburra was thumbing its nose at him again.

He thrust the bit and brace at Jenny. 'Please, sterilise these and let me know the moment they're ready.'

'Absolutely. On my way.' She walked briskly down the corridor.

Small steps. Do it step by step. 'Sarah, tube Jim now and bag him. The moment the other nurse arrives, I need you to scrub up with me.'

Her amber eyes narrowed slightly. 'But I'm needed to do the anaesthetic.'

I need you next to me; I need you to be my hands. 'The nurse can handle that under instruction, and the other nurse can be scout. You're assisting me.' He turned, not waiting for her to argue, not waiting to see the censure in her eyes. His heart pounded hard against his ribs as he punched open the door with his free hand.

Fear slashed at him from every side, ripping at his already shredded confidence.

He dragged in some steadying breaths as he leaned against the scrub sink. Focusing all his concentration on the small nailbrush, he went through the motions of scrubbing up, a familiar ritual that soothed, bringing the fear down to a dull anxiety.

A new nurse rushed into the scrub room. 'I'm Karen, Mr Harrison. What size gloves?'

Five minutes later he was gowned and gloved and standing in Theatre without his stick. For a brief moment time slowed and intensified. The ECG machine beeped. Jim lay unconscious on the table, the clear ET tube protruding from his mouth as Jenny rhythmically squeezed the airbag. Sarah, dressed in a green sterile gown, counted instruments and three sets of eyes turned and zeroed in on him.

Fiery pain shot through his leg. 'I need a stool.' Somehow it came out as a firm command rather than a howl of pain. His gut churned; he didn't feel in command. But he had to act it. 'Lower the table.'

Karen wordlessly produced the stool and arranged the table. Thick silence cloaked them all. He wanted to reassure everyone, help them all relax, but how could he? He had scant faith in himself—why should they believe in him? Dread settled over him like thick, suffocating fog.

He sat down and the pain in his leg subsided. Hell, next he'd need a sterilised cane.

Jenny had shaved Jim's head, clearing his temple of hair as well as the skin that ran parallel to his ear. Ryan picked up the local anaesthetic and placed it in Sarah's hand.

'Infiltrate here.' He ran a gloved finger over the area.

Sarah's eyes flashed at him over her mask, almost yelling, *You do it,* but she wordlessly followed his instructions, injecting the numbing fluid under the skin. She withdrew the needle and put the syringe down. She hesitated for a moment and then picked up the scalpel.

Relief spread through him like warm treacle. Solid. Reassuring. Sarah would make the incision. She wasn't going to make a fuss and insist he do it. She would follow his instructions just like last week when she'd inserted Jason's chest tube.

His heart rate slowed and for the first time since he'd found Jim collapsed on the floor he relaxed. He would get through this.

'Scalpel, Doctor.'

Cold metal slapped against his gloved palm, which had automatically opened at the familiar words. The weight of the scalpel holder pressed down on him as if it were ten tonnes of bricks. He stared down at the silver blade. Acid surged into his stomach.

He met Sarah's gaze, her eyes filled with an odd mixture of firmness, concern and belief. She wanted him to operate. Believed he could operate.

Jenny and Karen's eyes bored down on him, along with the weight of their expectation.

Jim's life hung in the balance.

He had no choice.

His hand slowly folded, encasing the thin metal handle. His knuckles gleamed white through the latex. He centred all his concentration on the scalpel. A wave of tension ricocheted through the muscles in his arm and hand. He breathed deeply.

Slowly, he brought the scalpel point to rest on Jim's temple.

His hand held steady.

Swallowing hard, he made a precise three-centimetre incision through the skin and fascia.

Relief cascaded through him. He was back in familiar territory. *One step at a time.* 'Retractor and gauze.'

Sarah applied the small retractor and controlled the bleeding. 'I thought it would bleed more.'

'The epinephrine in the local anaesthetic helps control the superficial bleeding. We'll need to cauterise the middle meningeal artery.'

She stood so close, her scent making his nostrils tingle, the fragrance flooding him with memories of fresh sunshine and summer flowers and spicy mint.

Her eyes crinkled around the edges, smiling at him as they peeked over her mask. 'You're doing really well.'

He strained to hear the muffled words behind the surgical mask, spoken quietly for his ears only. Her words bolstered him. He could do this.

Sarah passed him the drill.

He ran his gloved finger along the line halfway between the eye and the ear. 'The burr-hole is made two centimetres behind the orbital process of the frontal bone.' *And you drill carefully so you don't plunge into the brain.* The thought made him go rigid.

He gripped the brace, his breathing suddenly shallow. A slight tremor rippled through his arm and disappeared. Closing his eyes, he visualised the procedure. *One step at a time.*

Pulling on every skill he had, he blocked out all other thoughts, all other sounds. He slowly drilled through the outer table of the skull bone to the inner table.

'Cylindrical drill now?' Sarah's question broke though his self-imposed sound barrier.

'That's exactly what I need.' She was one hell of a GP.

He attached the bit. 'Get the diathermy ready and I'll need bone wax for the bone bleeding.'

He turned the brace handle until the resistance of the bone gave way. Using bone forceps, he carefully enlarged the opening.

As expected, blood gushed onto the sterile field. 'Diathermy.'

Sarah applied the tip of the diathermy to the artery. She moved slightly so her foot could press the pedal to engage the heat that would cauterise the area and stop the bleeding.

'Quickly, Sarah.' A prickle of unease ran through him.

'It's not working.' Her voice wobbled slightly. 'Karen, check the connection.'

Karen dived underneath the sterile drapes. 'It's all plugged in, no loose cables.' She fiddled at their feet. 'I've reconnected it—try it now.'

Sarah pressed down again.

Ryan waited for the tell-tale sizzle of the diathermy.

Alarm flashed in Sarah's eyes. 'Nothing.'

Adrenaline surged, his heart raced. 'Hell—get me 5.0 Silk, now! I'll have to tie it off.' That's all they needed, Jim bleeding out on the table. 'Suction.' He had to see where the bleeding was coming from.

'Doctors, his pressure's dropping.' Jenny's words increased the already palpable tension in the room.

The door of the supply cupboard slammed and Karen immediately opened the black suture thread onto the sterile tray. '5.0 Silk.'

'I'll keep it as clear as I can for you with the suction.' Sarah's voice steadied with returning control.

His blood pounded at his temples as he picked up the thread. *I can do this.* With extreme care he slid the black silk in place and prepared to tie off the bleeder. 'Suction.'

Sarah cleared the area of blood.

With forceps he pulled the thread ends together. *Left over right and under.* He lowered one end of the thread across the body to make a loop and reached with forceps to pull it through. *Halfway now. One step at a time.*

Without warning, a violent tremor ripped through his arm down to the tips of his fingers, scattering all control. His chest tightened. Sweat dripped into his eyes, blurring his focus.

He blinked furiously and pulled in a breath, forcing every ounce of concentration he had onto steadying his hand. He must complete the delicate tie and stem the bleeding.

He slowly turned the forceps, edging the tips together, millimetre by millimetre.

His fingers jerked.

The metal tips of the forceps clashed and he dropped the tie.

Jim's blood spurted out.

'More suction.' He heard his voice in the distance, as if it was coming from somewhere else.

Sarah's right hand immediately rested over his trembling one. She gently guided his hand to meet the forceps in his left hand.

Her firm pressure steadied his recalcitrant hand.

The ends met.

The knot tied.

The bleeding stopped.

Nausea rolled through him, almost making him gag.

Your competency is in doubt. What the hell had he been thinking?

The board was right. He shouldn't be operating.

'Hand syringe.' He forced his voice to work against a constricted throat.

She passed it to him. 'Your diagnosis was spot on— the haematoma's really clear. Jim's fortunate you needed more wood.'

He evacuated the blood clot with a steady hand, his tremor receding almost as fast as it had appeared.

'That blood clot would have killed Jim, wouldn't it?' Karen opened a dressing pack onto the sterile area. 'Thank goodness you were here, Mr Harrison.'

Jenny nodded. 'It's Jim and Yakkaburra's lucky day, that's for sure.'

'Yes, thank you.'

The unmistakable heartfelt tone in Sarah's softly spoken words washed over him. For a brief moment he savoured the delicious warmth that started to expand inside him at her praise.

You stuffed up!

Reality slammed him, dousing all warmth and approbation.

He could not let himself believe them. Their chatty style belied the whole situation. They acted as if as there'd been no crisis, no extreme danger to their patient, no surgeon fumbling at exactly the wrong moment.

Hadn't they seen him drop the ligature?

He didn't deserve this. Their praise, thanks and congratulations suddenly tasted bitter.

He was a danger to patients. No way was he risking another episode of the shakes.

With pristine clarity he knew exactly what he had to do.

Deliberately avoiding Sarah's eyes, he pushed his stool back, the wheels skating over the floor toward the bin. Stripping off his gloves, he summoned up a firm, loud voice from deep within, a tone that defied his true feelings. 'You close, Sarah. I need to ring the neurologist at Cairns hospital and chase down that helicopter.'

He stood up, bracing his stool against the wall. 'Jenny, as soon as I'm off the phone I'll be back to bring Jim around. Meanwhile, keep up the good work, team.'

He limped out of Theatre, hating his body that denied him an exit with a firm stride. Somehow he stumbled to the change room. The moment the door slammed behind him his façade of a surgeon in complete control crumpled, along with his body as he slid down the bank of lockers, his head in his hands.

Sarah wanted to sink into her couch at home and have a huge mug of restorative tea. But that wasn't an option just yet because she was still at work. Jim had been air-evacuated to Cairns, she'd seen to the paperwork, and Theatre was completely clean and tidy. Everything had been set to rights. It was as if the whole emergency had never happened.

But it had and the ripples of it would be felt for a long time.

She needed to talk to Ryan. Needed to debrief with him, for her sake as much as his. He'd done a brilliant job, considering it had been the first time he'd been in Theatre since his accident. He'd saved Jim's life.

Karen touched her shoulder. 'Sarah, we're going the pub to have a quiet drink. We're going to toast Jim and we want to thank Ryan in true Yakkaburra style.' She grinned. 'Bring him along when he's off the phone, OK?'

'Sure.' Sarah smiled. Jenny and Karen had risen to the occasion superbly. Neither of them had worked in Theatre for many years and they deserved to talk about the whole event in a casual environment.

'Great. And he can give us an update on Jim because he's talking to Roger Dunkley, the neurologist in Cairns, now.' Karen gave her a quick wave as she walked toward the door.

Sarah headed down the corridor and into the staff-room. Ryan sat with his legs stretched out straight in front of him. He spun his cane in his left hand while he spoke on the phone.

She'd noticed he often spun it or twirled it when he was sitting, used it as a pointer, even rested his hands and chin on it. It had become an extension of him despite his professed dislike of it. Deep lines of exhaustion scored the skin under his eyes. She knew how he felt.

She made two mugs of tea while he finished the call and then sat.

He snapped his mobile shut. 'Jim's stable, he's drowsy but making sense and his GCS is rising so it's all good news.'

He smiled as he picked up the steaming mug, his dimple seeming to dance against his cheek.

A rush of delicious tingling whipped through her, chasing away the stress of the day. She could gaze at that dimple for ever. 'That's the best news we could have hoped for and it's all because of you.'

Instantly, his dimple vanished. His mouth flattened, edged with hardness. 'Don't patronise me, Sarah.'

A jolt of anguish rushed through her at his unexpected words. 'I'm not patronising you. Why would you think that?'

He rubbed the back of his neck, the familiar gesture putting her on alert.

'You know as well as I do that I wasn't able to tie that ligature without your help.' A frown creased his high brow.

She sighed. She should have realised the man was a perfectionist. 'It was just one of those things. The situation shouldn't have even arisen but we've got old equipment. The diathermy failed and it was a fine tie complicated by a small space.'

He sat up ramrod straight. 'That's irrelevant. A surgeon has to deal with whatever unexpected things happen. I wasn't able to do that.'

Incredulity at his attitude rushed in. 'Are you going to focus on the *one* thing you struggled with and forget the way you more than competently dealt with the rest?' She heard her voice rising and tried to control it. 'You made a perfect incision. You evacuated the haematoma as if you did it every day.'

He grunted. 'I wasn't up to the job.'

She threw up her hands in frustration. 'You're not a brain surgeon or a plastic surgeon. Fine, delicate stitches are not expected of you.'

'I was known for my neat skin closures.' His icy voice tried to freeze her out.

She pushed on, trying to dent the barricades he'd erected. 'Today you had one tremor, and it disappeared quickly. All I did was give you a bit of support. Just like your surgical registrar would have done in Melbourne.'

'I *never* needed support.' He spoke through gritted teeth.

Her concern and frustration erupted into anger. How could the man be so obtuse? 'So you were a robot, were you? Well, welcome to the real world. You're human like the rest of us now. We make mistakes and we stuff up.' She dragged in a breath, trying to calm down. 'You didn't make a mistake today. You saved a man's life, doing emergency surgery outside your field of expertise.'

His eyes flashed and he opened his mouth but she refused to let him speak until she'd finished. 'There are a lot of people in Yakkaburra who want to thank you. I suggest you accept their thanks with grace and charm. Jim would be dead today if it wasn't for you and, like it or not, you have to accept that you're a hero in Yakkaburra.'

Suddenly exhaustion dumped on her like a wave at the beach. She'd tried and she'd hit a brick wall. Pushing her chair back, she stood up. 'I'm going to the pub to debrief with Jenny and Karen. At least they'll believe me when I thank them.'

She knew he would run back to his renovations so there was no point inviting him to the pub. Why put herself out there to be rejected again? It had taken her a long time but finally she was learning. It was best to leave him be. Best for both of them. She walked to the door.

'Sarah.'

Butterflies took flight as his rich baritone voice spoke her name. She turned slowly, trying to compose herself so she could casually look him in the eye like a colleague rather than a woman with a ridiculous crush. *Yeah, right.*

His eyes, which a few moments ago had flashed so indignantly, had a look of contrition mixed with something she couldn't identify. 'I'm sorry. I should have thanked you.' His formal tone faded. 'You did a great job today, both at the hardware store and in Theatre. You're a damn good GP.' His words sounded slightly husky in the silence of the room.

His unexpected praise, carried on the sexiest voice she'd heard, sent her blood rushing to her feet. Her knees started to shake. Confusion swirled with desire, creating a wall of heat that lit through her like wildfire with a north wind chaser. 'I... It was... I mean... Thank you...' The words faltered out. *Oh, God, I am such an idiot.*

She wished she could just evaporate there and then. Why did she become incoherent around him? How did the clock wind back so instantly to year twelve?

'Can I limp you to the pub?' He gave her a wry smile.

Her heart hammered so fast against her ribs she thought it would bounce out of her chest. That was the last thing she'd expected him to say. He was making a joke against himself. He wanted to come to the pub with her.

She wanted to dance around in silly circles and yell out, *Woo-hoo.*

He's not coming to be with you. He's coming to accept the thanks of the town, like you told him he should.

The bubble of joy inside her burst. 'Sure, that would be great. I'll just ring Sam at my mum's and say goodnight to him.'

This was her life. Single mother to Sam, country GP. Brooding surgeons with coal-black eyes played no role in it. And she was fine with that, wasn't she?

CHAPTER SIX

RYAN sat on the large couch in the Yakkaburra pub, wedged in by the other five people who had squeezed on the ends. Noise and conversation buzzed around him as people talked about the afternoon's drama.

Apparently everyone in town knew and admired Jim, and as Sarah had predicted, they all wanted to say thank you. The whole experience seemed surreal, none of it matching up with his childhood memories of Yakkaburra.

His back was bruised from the all congratulatory pats, and his hand tender from the many enthusiastic thank-you handshakes.

Sarah wriggled next to him. 'Sorry, Ryan, I'm squashing your leg.'

His heated blood raced to his groin. 'No, really you're fine.' Oh hell, even he could hear the hoarseness in his voice.

He forced himself to smile and take part in the general conversation but his concentration was constantly derailed by the delicious pressure of Sarah's leg against his own, the softness of her shoulder as it moved across the front of his chest when she leaned forward, and the showering sparks of sensation that raced into every part of him when her arm brushed the top of his leg.

The scent of her hair perfumed every breath he took. He longed to run his hand up her slender neck and into her thick, chestnut hair.

It was a completely insane idea. Thank goodness he was out in public, the perfect brake on his desire-fuelled instincts.

'My God, Ryan Harrison, how wonderful to see you again after all these years.'

The buzz of relaxed conversation around him instantly ceased. Sarah stiffened next to him. He turned toward the purring voice that sounded soft yet demanded complete attention.

A tall, elegant, immaculately dressed woman smiled at him, although the smile didn't quite reach her calculating eyes. His gut clenched. For a brief moment time rolled back. The girl he'd tried so hard to impress.

She'd led the power-hungry popular high-school set, the people who'd controlled who was in and who was out, who was tormented and who was accepted. *As if I'd kiss a loser like you.*

He pushed on his cane and rose to his feet so he could dwarf her with his height. *You're a grown-up now.* He stared down at this woman, the adult version of the girl who'd been part of the censorious Yakkaburra that had made his childhood hell, seeing for the first time the insecurity that drove her.

Drawing on the manners that had been ingrained in him by his grandmother, he extended his hand and kept his voice neutral, playing her words back to her. 'My God, Julie Lamond.'

She reached for his hand and shook it, her manicured fingers coolly curling around his hand, her thumb drawing a circle on his palm.

He extricated his hand, her touch making him feel slightly nauseous.

She perched herself on the large round arm of the opposite couch. Her short skirt rode up her gym-toned thighs as she crossed her legs, letting her designer sandal-clad feet dangle. 'I hear we have to thank you for saving our shopkeeper.' Her condescension clung to the last word.

Damn it—was this the woman he'd been so determined to impress by returning to Yakkaburra as a rich, successful surgeon? What the hell had he been thinking?

He sat down again between Sarah and Jenny, very aware of the tension that had entered their bodies the moment Julie had arrived. 'I had a great team so your thanks really need to go to Sarah, Karen, Jenny and Ron.' He swung his arm out to encompass the group.

Julie raised her brows and her words flirted. 'Yes, but you're the surgeon.' She turned her sights on Sarah and an edge entered her voice. 'Without Ryan, you would have been out of your depth.'

Fury ignited inside him. He couldn't believe after fifteen years this woman continued to play power games, and going by the silence of the group, it seemed the town still let her.

An overwhelming desire to protect surged through him. She could take potshots at him but not at Sarah. Before anyone spoke another word he waded in. 'Sarah is a damn fine GP and if I hadn't been here she would have done the same procedure with phone back-up from

Cairns.' He hooked his gaze to the ice-green stare of Julie's, staring her down. 'Yakkaburra is lucky to have her.'

'Of course we are.' She smiled sweetly, but her eyes glittered with a new hardness. 'It's so lovely to see the two of you getting along so well, considering how you deliberately overlooked her at school.' She stylishly slid to her feet. 'I'll catch up on all your news later when you're less occupied.'

She walked away, her gait reminding him of a snake slithering in the grass.

'That woman, honestly.' Jenny shook her head. 'She's as subtle as a sledgehammer. You better be careful, Ryan. She's recently divorced and on the lookout for a man. Snagging a surgeon would suit Councillor Lamond.'

Ryan laughed to cover the fact his brain was rehashing Julie's words *You deliberately overlooked her at school.* Hell, he couldn't even remember Sarah, so how could he have deliberately ignored her?

Sarah stood up, her face unusually pale with a rigid smile plastered on her face. 'I'd better head home. Thanks everyone, for your help today.'

Among the calls of 'Goodnight' and 'Thanks again', Ryan threw some money on the table. 'Have another round on me and get home safely.' By the time he'd struggled from the depths of the sagging couch, Sarah had disappeared.

A sense of urgency raced through him. Sarah had looked like she'd been kicked and he didn't want her to be alone. He had to find her and tell her that Julie Lamond wasn't worth the angst. Hell, he had enough experience of her bile to be an expert.

He came out of the front door of the pub and could see her determined figure striding quickly down the main street. He called out to her. 'Hey, Sarah, slow up a bit.'

She slowed slightly but didn't stop or speak.

He caught her up and walked along side her in silence. He wanted to speak but her waves of animosity kept crashing against him so he decided to wait until her anger faded a bit. Julie intentionally made people livid. She'd probably made Sarah's life hell and still was by the looks of it.

While he walked, he kept running scenes of his teenage years through his brain like spools of film, trying desperately to place Sarah. Julie's jibe about deliberately overlooked had to be a huge hint because that woman calculated every word she spoke. He must get hold of that school photo.

Sarah's usual vibrant energy, all positive and enthusiastic, had vaporised. Tension held every muscle rigid and she crossed her arms tightly against her chest, held her head erect and stared straight ahead.

They rounded the corner into their street, the silence of the night broken only by occasional coconuts dropping from the trees. He hadn't walked this far or this fast since before his accident and his leg burned with lactic acid and muscle fatigue. Every ounce of his energy had been absorbed trying to keep up with her.

She marched up her drive to the front door. Plunging her key into the lock, she wrenched the doorhandle to the right, and stomped inside.

He hesitated on the porch. Technically he'd walked her home safely but he couldn't leave her seething like this. He cautiously stepped inside and followed the noise of slamming kitchen cupboards. He leaned against the bench, facing her back. 'Don't let the likes of Julie Lamond get to you.'

She paused for a moment, intensely still. Then she slowly plugged in the automatic kettle and pressed the on switch, each action in the process precise and moderated.

Abruptly, she whirled around, her wrath exploding out of her like shot from a gun. 'You made me look like a child back there. I'm a big girl, Ryan Harrison. I don't need you to defend me.'

Her words hit him. All this time he'd thought she was furious with Julie, not him. 'But she openly ran you down.'

'Yes, she did, but if you'd given me a chance I would have dealt with her in my way. The way I always do, have always done.' Her usually smiling, lush, kissable mouth was a firm line. Uncompromising.

He shifted his weight, bewilderment skating through him, unable to get a foothold for clarity. 'Her comment got under my skin. No one makes a crack at my team and gets away with it.'

Sarah bit her lip, confusion swimming in her eyes, backlit by hope. 'Your team?'

He shrugged, trying to make light of his previous words, wanting to lessen the chance Sarah might think he'd changed his mind and would work with her at the clinic. He tried to make a joke out of it. 'Today I had a team. No one messes with my team.'

He gave her a wry smile. 'I'm sorry I jumped in. Of course you can defend yourself, that was never in doubt.'

He ran his hand through his hair and continued, 'But that woman presses buttons. Julie specialises in power by humiliation. I remember how she ruled at school. Surely she's not still ruling the town?'

Sarah placed cups on the bench. 'She tries, but since her divorce her star is fading. She's lost a lot of alliances, things change.' She paused for a moment. 'People grow up, Ryan.'

He heard censure in her voice. 'What are you saying, that I'm stuck in the past?'

She looked at him, her perfect almond-shaped eyes glowing with battle-worn resignation. 'Well, as far as Yakkaburra is concerned, I think you are.'

Her attitude of 'Miss Well-Adjusted' niggled at him. 'So you're saying that nothing happened to you at high school that still comes back to bite you?'

She stiffened. 'Nothing.' The words snapped out too fast.

So she *was* hiding something. Without thinking, he closed the gap between them. He was so close he could hear her breathing, could see the flutter of a pulse in her neck. Her eyes mesmerised him, shimmering the colour of ripe, golden wheat as they valiantly held his gaze.

'Nothing at all?'

She swallowed hard and flicked her head so her jaw jutted. 'No.'

The need to touch her jolted him to his toes, while her slender neck taunted him. His fingers caressed her skin, tilting her chin ever so slightly, the contact sending heat thudding through him. 'Liar.' The word came out on a gravelly whisper.

She swayed slightly, her hair falling forward, making her look young and vulnerable.

God, she was gorgeous.

Kiss her.

No way. Hell, he didn't even know what the situation was with Sam's father. Right now his life was complicated enough, without kissing Sarah again.

A flash of a memory, indistinct and hazy—a shy smile, swirling long hair—hovered for a moment then faded, tantalising and elusive.

Sarah's lips parted as she took in a breath.

Desire, hot and strong, tore through him. Every good intention fled. He lowered his lips toward hers, needing to taste her, desperately wanting the connection, wanting to banish the past and delay the future.

He took it slowly, savouring the heat of her body against his, the way the fabric of her blouse moved across his palm as his hand cupped her waist, the soft press of her breasts on his chest—the feel of Sarah.

His lips swept lightly across hers, coaxing, calling her to join him.

Her lips met his, a pillow of welcoming softness. A moan sounded in her throat.

His control slipped a notch at the sound. His hand tightened at her waist, his tongue sought entry to her mouth. Velvet warmth encased him and he lost himself there, absorbed in the dance of the kiss. Everything in his life receded, except for the touch of her mouth against his.

Her taste of wine and fruit infused him as she leaned into the kiss, the pressure of her fingers digging into his arms as she steadied herself.

An image thudded into his brain, sharp and clear—the noise of a party, a blindfold, long brown hair and a mind-blowing kiss.

Sarah Rigby.

The quiet girl who'd always had her head in a book, the girl who'd smiled shyly in the corridor but had rarely spoken. She'd retreated into the background of high-school life. The girl he'd completely failed to notice.

Except for that one time.

He pulled back in shock, his memory of her so vivid, now displayed in 3D. Realisation thudded into him. 'I've kissed you before.'

Sarah struggled to focus on Ryan through a desire-fuelled haze while her stalled brain desperately tried to kick-start itself. 'Yes, you kissed me last week.' Her tongue darted out, moistening her lips, swollen from his amazing kisses.

'No, I mean I've kissed you before, a long time ago.' He stroked her hair. 'You had long hair down to your waist and you wore glasses.'

Oh, God, he'd remembered. Embarrassment swirled inside her, settling next to humiliation, which already sat heavily in her gut. She'd wanted him to remember her, remember their conversations, *not* that particular memory. It wasn't a good memory, it left her vulnerable.

She tried to keep her voice light, 'You thought I was Julie Lamond.' The words came out flat. She moved, planning to step out of his arms.

His hand firmed on her waist, holding her close, while he adjusted his weight against the bench. 'I thought you kissed like an angel.'

She pressed her forefinger firmly against his chest, unable to keep fifteen years of hurt inside her. 'You ran out of the house with a look of pure horror on your face.'

He tilted his head, understanding dawning. 'Is there a statute of limitations on apologies for stupid things you did as a teenager?' The darkness of his eyes softened. 'I didn't mean to hurt your feelings. Me leaving had nothing to do with you and everything to do with Julie. I was so furious with her. She'd set me up and I'd played into her hands.'

Delight whizzed around her. He hadn't been horrified at the discovery he'd been kissing her. *Me leaving had nothing to do with you.* It was silly to feel such a sense of relief at his words fifteen years after the event, but she did.

Thankfully, the secret of her crush for him all that time ago was still safe. 'That party was the last time I saw you until three weeks ago.'

His hand kneaded her back. 'I left town that night. I'd been planning on leaving but that pushed me out a few days early. I'd officially had enough.'

His warm breath played across her face. She wanted to stay in his arms but he'd been standing for a long time. She picked up his hand and moved toward the couch. 'We should sit down.'

'Thanks.' He gave her a grateful smile, his dimple flashing as he sat and stretched out his leg.

How could a smile reduce her to such a quivering mess? 'So seeing Julie tonight brought it all back?'

'Yeah.' He nodded. 'I had this crazy plan that if I dated Julie, the town's attitude toward my family and me would change. I'd get the acceptance I craved and Yakkaburra would forget that my mother was an alcoholic and my father had scarpered.'

She remembered all the whispered adult conversations about the Harrisons in the past, and now it all made sense. She ached when she thought of the childhood he must have had, so very different from her own. 'But the plan didn't work.'

He shrugged. 'It was doomed from the start but when you're a kid and desperate, you try anything.' His onyx eyes suddenly lit up as a thought struck him. 'Hey, if I thought I was kissing Julie Lamond, who did you think you were kissing?'

The creeping heat in her cheeks started the moment she heard his question. *Relax.*

But it was too late. She was officially hopeless, a grown woman who still blushed. No way was she telling him the truth. A reignited crush after fifteen years and a failed marriage made her look ridiculous. She airily waved a hand. 'Oh, some boy I had a crush on, I can't remember.'

He swung his arm casually along the back of the couch, his fingers tantalisingly close to her shoulder. His eyes danced with wicked intent. 'I don't believe you.'

'Hey, it's taken you three weeks to remember me. I think I can have a forgotten crush.' Her heart hammered hard in her chest. He was too close to the truth.

The deepness of his voice washed over her. 'Everything Julie does has a calculated motive.'

'True.' She swallowed, trying to keep her concentration on his words rather than the closeness of his body.

'So, based on her comment at the pub…'

His fingers caressed her shoulder, sending shafts of pleasure to every part of her.

'I think that night you knew you were kissing me.'

Her breath caught in her throat. He couldn't know.

Forcing herself to laugh, she pushed her hand hard against his chest in an uncharacteristic, flirty gesture. 'Oh, get over yourself.'

Quickly, his hand captured hers and he brought it to his mouth, his lips gently pressing against her palm.

The tenderness of the action sent quivers of longing sweeping through her. She wanted to hold onto that feeling for ever.

All too quickly he lowered her hand, placing it in her lap, and then released his fingers.

Loss pierced her. She wanted his touch. It had been so long since she'd been caressed like that. Way before David had died.

His laughter lines smoothed over, his dimple flattened out into the flat plane of his cheek, his expression now serious. 'Fair enough, but what about now? What about this thing that hovers between us?'

She knew exactly what he meant. When they were together the air seemed charged, every action heightened, and her awareness in overdrive. And the kisses they'd shared eclipsed every kiss she'd ever received.

But his life was in flux and she needed to give Sam stability. 'I guess it hovers.'

His jaw tightened. 'Because of Sam's father?'

His question puzzled her. 'What does David have to do with it?'

'You tell me.' His face had changed from open to thunderous and closed.

What had upset him so much? Past conversations ran through her head. Anything personal they'd talked about had really been about him. She closed her eyes, realisation dawning. She'd never talked about David to him.

She never talked about David to anyone. When she'd said, "I guess it hovers," he'd thought she was still married.

Her stomach churned. She didn't want to talk about David. David was the past, her biggest mistake. But Ryan thought he must still be in her life.

She couldn't let him think that she would stoop so low as to still be married and yet be kissing him. 'David died a few years ago.'

He sat back in the couch, distancing himself from her, regret clearly shining from his eyes. 'Oh, God, I'm sorry.'

Her chest tightened at his awkwardness. This was why she hated talking about David. People gave her sympathy and she didn't deserve it.

She took in a long, slow breath, steadying herself to explain. 'David and I were pretty much at the pretend stage of happy families when he died in a car accident.' She sighed. 'Being considered his grieving widow is even harder, it feels so dishonest.'

Understanding replaced the awkwardness. 'Accepting sympathy for a loss you don't feel as intensely as people imagine would be tough.'

His insight was spot on. 'Yeah.' She stood up. 'I think I'll make that tea now.' She'd told him enough. Hiding out in the kitchen seemed like a good idea.

A few moments later Ryan's hand closed gently around her arm. 'Sarah, I'll make the tea. You sit at the bench, it sounds like you need to talk.'

Indignation rushed through her. 'I don't need to talk about it! I was married, now I'm not, end of story.'

He raised his brows as he re-boiled the kettle. 'O-K.'

She crossed her arms, wanting to be petulant, wanting to stay mute. What did he know?

He's been through a life-changing event. Perhaps he learned that talking helps.

She hated her rational self. She'd never told anyone about her sham of a marriage, not even her mother. For years she'd held in her disappointment and pain. Then David's death had compounded her feelings, adding guilt to the mix.

It was all a damn mess.

A photo of a four-year-old Sam with David caught her eye. Sam must have been looking at it and forgotten to take it back to his room. She picked it up, running her finger along the frame.

Her indignation at Ryan ran out of steam. 'Sam is the one who deserves the sympathy. He lost his dad.' Old tension coiled inside her. 'Actually, he lost the idea of a dad.'

Ryan slowly turned the teapot three times before pouring the tea, his expression unusually neutral. 'Wasn't David around much?'

'His priorities lay elsewhere.' She stirred the tea even though she took it black with no sugar, the action releasing some of her agitation. 'His job and his perceived place on the social ladder took precedence. Sam and I always came a poor second.'

Ryan released a hiss of breath and tilted the photo, his fingers brushing hers with a feather-like touch. 'He looks familiar.'

She stomped on the crazy, skittering feeling that danced through her at his brief touch. 'You would have seen him on television or billboards.' She put on a *faux* deep voice. "Tonight on *Medical Moments*, Dr David Delahunty explains liposuction."

'You don't sound like you approved of his career choice.' Ryan pushed a plate of biscuits toward her.

'Put it this way, being a celebrity suited David but it didn't suit us.' She spun off the chair and headed back to the other room, needing to pace. Her heart pounded. She'd started this story so she'd have to finish. But she wanted to stop. Wanted to go back to ignoring her life with David and leave the past in the past.

Telling the rest would only expose herself for the fool she was when it came to men. And exposing herself to the one man whose opinion of her she valued terrified her.

Ryan watched Sarah stare out the window, the moonlight washing over her in a pool of soft white light. She looked petite and vulnerable. The confident woman he knew had faded in front of his eyes. For the first time he saw glimpses of the teenage Sarah. Her rigid shoulders, the constant movement of her hands—every action screamed that her body and emotions were at war. He'd bet his last dollar she'd not told anyone this story before.

She's in pain—do you really need to know?

But this was more than curiosity. If he was right, she'd bottled up these feelings for too long; she needed to let them out. And he needed to listen.

He pulled out a dining chair and sat down. 'What happened, Sarah?' His voice sounded loud in the quietness of the room.

She spoke with her back to him. 'What didn't happen? It was partly my fault. I should have recognised the type of person David was but I was a small-town girl in the big city with virtually no experience.' She turned to stare straight at him. 'Apart from one kiss.'

One kiss she'd remembered and he'd let the associated anger and hurt push it out of his mind. 'Hey, it was a great kiss.'

'Yeah, right, you really remembered it.' She gave a half-laugh. 'I must have been the only virgin at the end of six years of uni in Brisbane. I had a large group of friends and I was flat out studying so I really had no one to compare David to.'

She sat on the wide window-sill, half facing him, half facing the night. 'First Sydney dazzled me, and then David. He could charm a chair and his charisma was legendary. Only I didn't know that and I fell for him without knowing I was part of his grand plan.'

An ache ran up his jaw and he realised he was gritting his teeth. The more he heard about this guy, the less he liked. He hated it that Sarah's usual self-assurance seemed shaky, that just talking about David seemed to drain her. 'Grand plan?'

She grimaced. 'It was a toss-up who David loved more, himself or money. As the top student of my year he saw I had brains and he equated that with earning capacity. Two consultants working full time would give him the disposable income to live the life he coveted— fast cars, designer clothes and a harbour-side home.'

Ryan must have missed something. None of this sounded like the Sarah he knew. 'Two consultants? I thought you were a GP?'

'I am. That was the start of things going sour. I'd let David railroad me and I'd been accepted into the cardiology programme. But three months in I discovered I was pregnant. I was thrilled. David was underwhelmed.' Her bitterness clouded her eyes, rolling in like a sea fog.

He had to ask—surely this poor excuse for a man hadn't insisted on a termination. 'And this baby was Sam?'

She nodded, some of the bitterness fading. 'I took maternity leave, wanting to be a hands-on parent. When Sam turned six months, David started applying a lot of pressure for me to return to cardiology. He hated the constraints one income put on his lifestyle.'

He beat down the unexpected anger that surged inside him.

'And did you?'

'No, I held out and worked a few sessions a week as a GP, to keep the debt in check.' She grimaced. 'The debt I'm still paying off. It was worse than rocky there for a bit but then David picked up the *Medical Moments* gig. That took the pressure off me.' Her voice sounded tired, defeated. 'Being a celebrity doctor was beyond his wildest dreams and he started to live life as if he was well established in both media and medicine.'

He couldn't help frowning, unable to hide his inherent dislike of her now deceased husband who had failed her so badly. 'Why didn't you leave him?'

She pulled her knees up under her chin and shivered despite the warmth of the night. 'I couldn't walk away from the marriage so soon after it had started. I believed I had to make it work for Sam's sake.'

She turned and caught his gaze. 'He deserved a father. Besides, image was everything to David and divorce wouldn't look good so early in his media career.' She signed. 'So we led separate lives under the same roof. He wanted fame and pursued that. I focused on Sam.'

He ached for her. She deserved so much more. 'You're doing a great job with Sam.'

She hugged her legs close to her chest. 'Sam is the *one* thing I don't regret about my time with David. He's the reason I'm back in Yakkaburra.' Her voice trembled. 'He lost his dad, but at least he has his grandparents.'

He wanted to haul her into his arms, comfort her and tell her not to be so hard on herself. But she'd thrown a no-go zone up around herself. Something that hadn't existed until she'd started to talk about her husband.

'And what about you?'

'I'm a lot wiser now. I'm busy with work and Sam, it's all I need.' She threw him a silencing look, a don't-go-there stare. Pushing herself to her feet, she tossed her head as if her hair was still long. Immediately he knew she'd just made a decision. 'Ryan, it's been a long day and I'm exhausted.'

Frustration and disappointment flooded him. He was being sent home. Packed off, instructed not to act on their attraction. He lurched to his feet and walked to the front door, wondering where he stood with her. Not a colleague. Certainly *not* a lover. Friend? He swallowed a sigh and tried to keep his tone light. 'Tell Sam to come over tomorrow after school if he wants to. I'm sanding the floors.'

She shot him a look of pure incredulity, immediately followed up by dismay, and wordlessly closed the door behind him.

His dismissal was complete.

The feeling totally sucked.

CHAPTER SEVEN

'I WONDER if my dad was as good as you are at fixing things.'

Ryan and Sam munched on cake and drank cordial, taking a break from sanding the floors. Earlier in the day, Ryan had made yet another attempt at his grandmother's 'no-fail' chocolate cake recipe. He was improving but this version had a definite dip in the middle. Still, that made the centre deliciously gooey with rich chocolate.

Sam's statement surprised him. He hadn't really mentioned his father much, although he often spoke about his grandfather and his current male teacher.

As good as you are at fixing things. Delight tripped through him at the young boy's words. He'd never thought of himself as handy or as a renovator, but he loved every minute of the work. Deep down a sense of pride warmed him. He'd achieved a lot in the past few weeks. The veranda was slowly coming back to its Edwardian glory and as soon as Jim was back on his feet, he'd ask him to chase up the patterned glass panels for the veranda doors.

He looked at his eager helper. As much as he didn't like the sound of David Delahunty, Sam saw him as a hero and he had to respect that. 'Everyone has a talent and a skill. If your dad wasn't that great at fixing things then he'd have been great at something else.'

Sam looked thoughtful. 'He got a trophy for basketball.'

'There you go. Sounds like he was good at sport, just like you.'

He beamed. 'Can you play sport?' His hopeful voice was at odds with the expression on his face as he glanced at Ryan's scarred leg.

A shard of regret cut into him. Regret that Sam hadn't known him when he'd been whole. Still, he'd been surprised at the strength his leg had gained in the last month, considering the plateau it had stalled on since the end of his rehabilitation. 'I'm not quite up to basketball yet, but I love body-boarding.'

'Oh, cool! Mum and I go to this great beach. It doesn't have big surf but Mum likes coming in on the small waves.' His shoulders slumped slightly. 'But she always wants to get out of the surf before I do.' He paused for a moment and then his face became wreathed in a smile. 'Hey, you should come with us.'

A vision of a laughing Sarah, riding a board in a red bikini, slammed into him. His mind blanked. Heat coursed through him, sending an intense longing into every crevice and cranny.

'Ryan?' Sam queried. 'Want to come with us?'

The child's voice broke though his lust, bringing him quickly back to the present with a healthy dollop of guilt. Lusting after the kid's mother in front of the kid wasn't something he was proud of.

He tried to force the image out of his head by replacing the bikini with a neck-to-knee wetsuit. *Worse!*

He breathed deeply. 'If Mum is OK with it, sure, I'd love to come.'

Sam jumped to his feet. 'I'll go ask her.'

Ryan caught Sam's arm. 'Hold on, sport. Mum's busy at work so you can ask her at teatime.'

Sam's shoulders slumped. 'I guess.'

Ryan's heart shredded slightly at Sam's dejected look. It was very hot and had been for days. He was sick of breathing in polyurethane fumes and dust. And Sam had been a willing helper so he deserved a treat. Hell, so did he.

He hadn't seen Sarah in person since she'd closed the door behind him nine nights ago. But he'd seen her vividly every night in his dreams.

He missed her smile, her laugh and the way her brow furrowed at the bridge of her nose when she concentrated. He wanted to see her again. Needed to see her again. 'What about we ditch our overalls, get a picnic together and pick Mum up from work and go to this beach?'

Sam's eyes rounded to perfect circles. 'Really?'

He leaned back in his chair. 'Why not? It's Friday, there's no school tomorrow so Mum will let you have a late night, won't she?'

'Yippee!' Sam pushed his hand in the air. 'I'll go get my board and my bathers and sunscreen and Drover. Drover can come 'cos he loves the beach and we can take a ball and he'll fit in your car, right?'

Ryan pictured his two-door sports car with a salty, sandy dog in the back and tried not to cringe. But you couldn't organise a surprise picnic and ask to use the suprisees' minivan. 'Pack a huge sheet and towel for Drover.'

* * *

'Have a good weekend, Jenny.' Sarah called goodbye as she left the building, clutching her medical bag, which had become a permanent extension of herself.

The beep of a horn made her turn. Sam came barrelling out of Ryan's car. 'Mum, Mum, we've packed a picnic and we're going to the beach.' He raced up to her, panting hard, and grabbed her hand. 'Come on.'

Ryan stood next to the open passenger door, tall and tanned. His relaxed face grinned back at her and the deep lines of pain around his eyes that had been so marked a month ago were less pronounced.

Her heart kicked over. He thought his body damaged but about that he was clueless. His muscled shoulders filled his shirt and his rounded biceps bulged out of the short sleeves. Her imagination filled in the blanks of the six-pack that lay underneath his polo shirt. His good leg was solid muscle, and even his damaged leg had more definition than when he'd first arrived.

The teenage Ryan Harrison had been defined by the brooding looks that had belonged to a biker, a renegade who'd left town not giving a damn. Since he'd been back in Yakkaburra he'd pretty much been uptight and defensive.

But today, as he leaned against his insanely expensive car, filled incongruously with a devoted kelpie, panting out of the window, he had a calmness about him. Calmness surrounded by an aura of devilment.

His black hair, now speckled with stress-induced grey, gleamed in the sun and midnight black eyes twinkled at her, daring her to go along with this spur-of-the-moment plan.

He'd never looked sexier.

And that scared her to death.

'It's time to put the week behind you. Your transport to Kirikiki Beach awaits.' He swept his hand in front of him, indicating she should get into the car.

She focused on slowing her hammering heart. She reminded herself she was cross with him. Cross with him for treading water with his life, cross with him for not coming to work at the clinic.

Cross with herself for missing his company so much over the last week.

She pressed her hands against her work trousers. 'I'm hardly dressed for the beach.'

Sam rolled his eyes. 'We packed your towel, your bathers and your body-board.'

A vision of Ryan standing in her bedroom, looking for bathers as he sorted through her drawer of lacy underwear, to find her bathers, almost made her stagger.

A deep, wicked laugh boomed around her as he caught her horrified expression. 'Sam did the clothes packing and I looked after the food.'

He saw right through her. Every time.

Sam's excited hand tugged at her own. 'Hurry up, Mum.'

She looked down at her son's face, filled with the joy of an outing to his favourite beach. She glanced into Ryan's relaxed face, which showed absolutely no signs of the tortured man she ached for. She couldn't deny either of them this outing.

She laughed. 'I hope you packed a lot of food because I'm starving.'

Sam scrambled into the car behind the passenger

seat and she hopped in. Ryan closed her door and then walked around the car, his limp less pronounced.

He reversed and headed the car out of town and toward the coast.

Sam chattered away about school and what he'd been helping Ryan do at the house until he'd exhausted all he wanted to say. Then he starting his usual pass-the-time game of counting off each of the landmarks that told him he was getting closer to the beach.

The silence in the car wrapped Sarah in a bubble of comfort and she leaned back, sneaking sideways glances at Ryan, whose dark eyes were hidden behind designer sunglasses, similar to David's.

A slight ripple of unease ran through her. *He's nothing like David. His car and sunglasses are just left-overs from his life before the accident.* Unlike David, he'd reined in his spending when his income had dropped. She was still paying off David's debt.

She shook her head. She didn't want to think about David, so she blurted out the first thought that came into her mind. 'It's great news about Jim, isn't it?'

'What's the update?' Ryan flicked the visor down against the glare of the late afternoon sun.

'He's going to be discharged this weekend.' She shifted sideways to look at him properly. 'Roger Dunkley said he'd rung you.'

'I must have missed his call.' His jaw tightened for a moment.

She raised her brows. 'You probably couldn't hear the phone over the roar of the sander.'

His head snapped around and for a brief moment his eyes sparked. 'We're both off duty, Sarah, and this is Sam's picnic.'

She nodded, biting back her snippy reply. She hated that she'd let her frustration push him. He'd rightfully chastised her—now was not the time or place. Why was it so hard for her to accept his reluctance to go back to work?

Because it's such a waste. The voice yelled loudly in her head before she stuffed it back into its box.

'So, Sam…' She swivelled round to see him and her face almost collided with Drover's tongue. A two-door sports car meant not much space between the back and the front seats. 'How much further?'

'We've passed the Cassowary Crossing signs, the turn-off to the Crocodile Adventures and the gate of the Aboriginal Dance Company.' Sam ticked off the landmarks on his fingers. 'So that only leaves the little shop and we're there.'

She turned back and pointed to the brown tourist sign up ahead. 'You need to turn at the next intersection.'

Ryan activated the indicator. 'Why do you come all the way down to this beach?'

'Stinger net.' Sarah grimaced. 'Nothing spoils a day at the beach like needing antivenom and a two-hour ride to Cairns hospital.'

'Plus, the beach is great for playing cricket,' Sam added.

'Sam's got his priorities sorted.' Ryan laughed, the sound one of sheer enjoyment.

A wave of pleasure swept through her and she joined in, letting herself totally relax. She hadn't felt this carefree for a long time.

Ryan parked the car and sat for a moment, staring out to sea at the string of islands that framed the horizon. He'd been in the south for so long that he'd forgotten the amazing turquoise of the water, so clear you could almost count the fish. No southern tea-tree here, just rainforest on the shoreline, palm trees swaying in the breeze and fallen coconuts washing up as sea-drift, resting on the golden sand.

He turned to Sarah but she was already out of the car. Sam and Drover were charging down the beach, sand flying, filled with the sheer joy of being outside on one of the world's most beautiful beaches. Drover, prancing with excitement, watched eagerly as Sam threw a stick into the water.

The moment the stick left the child's hands, the dog bounded into the surf, his head just above the small waves, and snatched the stick, bringing it straight back to his master.

If Ryan could interpret Drover's barks, he was certain the words would be "Again, again!"

He eased himself out of the car, using his stick, eager to join the fun.

He unloaded the boot and Sarah reappeared. The professional doctor in her black trousers, white shirt and heeled shoes had disappeared. In her place stood a barefoot woman, wearing a turtle-print sarong wrapped low on her hips. An expanse of tanned skin nailed his gaze, like a kangaroo caught in headlights. Low cut, sky-blue Lycra moulded itself to her breasts, pushing them together and creating a tantalising cleavage.

His mouth went dry.

'Do you need a hand carrying some gear?' She put her clothes in the boot and looked up at him, her expression helpful, the neighbourly Sarah, the Sarah who knew he hated not being able to use two hands when walking.

Helpful and incredibly hot. Hell. She had no idea of the effect she had on him.

He swallowed hard. 'I'll take the boards if you take the food bag.'

She smiled her wide, welcoming smile. 'Done.'

He tried to squash the surge of hunger her smile created. He followed her down to the beach, enjoying the view of her sarong shifting across her cute behind. *Bad idea. That won't squash it.*

'Hey, Sam, let's surf!' Ryan tossed his stick to Sarah and paddled out to sea, enjoying the cool, refreshing water on his way-too-aroused body.

The offshore islands meant the waves were fun but safe. Sam was a natural in the water and managed to catch even the smallest waves. As the tide started to change, the swell increased. Sarah paddled out to join them. She and Sam egged each other on, laughing and teasing.

He let the waves and water wash over him, enjoying every moment. A larger wave scooped him forward and suddenly he felt two hands on his back. Sarah's dancing eyes met his gaze on the left and Sam's freckled face grinned at him on his right. A wave of peace rolled through him.

Here and now he was just Ryan.

No pain, no expectations, no disappointment.

Contentment washed over him as the surf carried them to shore together.

'Come on, Mum, let's do it again.' Sam tucked his board under his arm and turned to head out again.

'I need food!' Sarah ran up the beach, rivulets of salty

water cascading off her body, over her breasts, down over her slightly rounded stomach, the badge of motherhood.

Ryan stayed in the water a moment longer.

As he stood, Sarah jogged back with a towel and his stick. 'Need this?' Her voice teased.

He grinned at her, high on the endorphins of exercise and her company. 'Let's see if I do.'

He took a step forward, gingerly putting his weight on his weaker leg. It held. He took a second step, the muscles tightened.

Sarah's hand hovered near his arm but her face was alive with excitement at his achievement. 'Hey, look at you.'

It spurred him on. He took a third and fourth step. The muscles burned and his leg trembled. 'Stick,' he rasped out the words impossible to keep back any longer.

She immediately pushed it into his hand, the metal handle hot against his palm. 'Sorry, Ryan, I shouldn't have pushed you.'

He held her arm and looked into anxious, amber eyes. 'You didn't push. An amazing thing just happened. I took five steps without my cane. That's never happened before.' His hand slipped into hers. 'You once told me small steps. I'm just following instructions.'

Sam and Drover belted past them, sand flying. 'Are you two coming? I'm starving.'

She squeezed his hand before letting it go and racing Sam up the beach. 'Don't touch that piece of chocolate cake, it's got my name on it.'

He followed them, almost floating up the beach on the euphoria of pushing through a personal barrier. Of being able to share that moment with this family.

Sharing it with Sarah.

He couldn't deny the exhilaration. And today he didn't want to. Sarah made him feel alive. He'd take today while it was on offer and just enjoy it.

It didn't take them long to eat all the food, their bodies craving fuel after all the exercise. Ryan stretched out on his towel, warm from the sun, warm from the food and warm from Sam and Sarah's company.

Sam had taken Drover back to the water for some more stick-retrieving. Ryan rolled on his side to look at Sarah, who lay with her eyes closed, savouring the rays of the setting sun.

Her long, dark lashes curled up from her smooth cheeks and salt glistened white on her skin.

An image rocked him, his tongue on her skin, licking the salt away. He rolled over.

This was ridiculous. With every passing moment he wanted her more. He wanted to take her in his arms and kiss her until her eyes were wide black discs of desire, her skin was blush pink with longing, her breath was ragged with yearning and she just melted against him, her legs weak with need.

But this was a family picnic and he needed to keep a lid on things.

'What are you thinking about?' Sarah's voice, languid with relaxation, broke into his wayward thoughts.

'Families.' He managed to croak out the words.

'Association of ideas?' She smiled.

They'd put you in jail for that association. 'What do you mean?'

She rolled over to face him and to keep an eye on Sam. 'My family are a beach family. As a kid we always had picnics at the beach, we went sailing, snorkelling, surfing. You name it, if it was associated with the water, we did it.' She ran sand through her fingers. 'Our neighbours always headed inland to the rainforest and went bushwalking and bird-watching. What was your family's tradition?'

Drinking bourbon until the pain went away. He had a sudden desire to tell Sarah the truth about his parents, it seemed right. 'My mother had no ability or energy for traditions. She was sixteen when she got pregnant with me. By the time I was old enough to have memories, my father had left town and my mother was pretty much drunk most of the time.'

He gave her a wry smile. 'But my grandmother loved me. She raised me, encouraged me and by sheer force of will kept me at school so I completed year twelve. I guess our annual Christmas trip to Cairns to visit her sister was our tradition.'

Her smile came with understanding, empathy and decisiveness. 'You'll just have to make up for lost time, then.'

Before he could ask her what she meant, she called Sam.

He ran up the beach, Drover at his heels, and skidded to a stop on his knees. 'What, Mum?'

Sarah slung her arm around Sam's shoulder. 'This is Ryan's first beach picnic.'

'No way.' He swung around to look at Ryan. 'Really?'

He laughed at Sam's uncomprehending expression. 'Really.'

Sarah stood up. 'So, we've been surfing and we've had our food mixed with flies and sand and there's not enough wind left for kite-flying, so that only leaves one thing to show him at this beach.'

'Cricket!' Sam dived for his bat. 'I'll be your runner, Ryan.'

The serious look of consideration on the boy's face touched him, and the permanent empty place inside him unexpectedly shrank a little. 'Thanks, mate.'

'And, Mum, you can bowl and Drover will help you field.' He dragged the bag down to the hard sand, exposed by the low tide.

'Come on, then. We've been organised so we better get cracking. It's serious stuff, this cricket.' She laughed as she untied her sarong, dropping it onto the towel.

This time he didn't bother to hide his appreciative gaze.

She blushed and then put her hands on her hips. 'I can't beat you if I'm hampered by a skirt.'

'Beat me, eh? I played cricket at uni.' He stood up and reached for her but she'd pulled away, laughing as she ran down to Sam's sand pitch.

Sam handed him the bat and whispered conspiratorially. 'Mum mostly bowls like a girl but now and then she sends down a yorker so be ready.'

Ryan kept a straight face and accepted the proffered bat with the seriousness appropriate to the occasion.

Sarah walked down the beach, turned and started to run in preparation to bowl.

Her toned legs ate the sand, her breasts moved against the Lycra and her hair swirled around her face.

She was all vibrant energy, life-affirming and totally gorgeous. His gaze was glued to her.

He swung and connected with air.

Sam grunted in disgust.

Reality centred Ryan. 'Sorry, mate. The next one will fly.' He stamped the bat onto the sand, his stance that of a professional cricketer. Closing his mind to everything except the ball, he swung, connected with it on the full and sent it blasting through the air.

Drover barked and tore down the beach. Sarah dashed across the sand, her arms out, anticipating a catch.

A cry of pain rent the air and she unexpectedly crumpled to the sand.

Ryan's gut clenched in apprehension. 'Sam, run to Mum. I'm coming.'

Sam's hesitated a moment, his face pale, and then ran to Sarah.

Ryan half strode, half limped to her, running through the possibilities that had caused her to fall. Sprained ankle, wasp sting, stubbed toe…

Sarah clutched her foot with her hand as bright red blood gushed out, seeping through the spaces between her fingers.

All colour had drained from her face and her eyes seemed larger than usual in her oval face. 'Cut my foot.' The words came out on a staccato beat.

Damn, he wasn't wearing his shirt and he needed something to stop the bleeding. 'Sam, go grab Mum's sarong and bring it fast as you can.'

The boy responded to the urgent tone in his voice and sprinted up the beach.

'Keep holding it as tight as you can. I don't want to examine it until I've got a pressure bandage.' Ryan knelt down next to her. 'What cut you?'

'Glass.'

Fury at the thoughtlessness of people surged through him.

'Here it is.' Sam panted as he passed the sarong to

Ryan. Then he threw his arms around Sarah, his face creased with worry.

'I'm OK, Sam, I just cut my foot.' Her voice sounded falsely jolly as she leaned against his little body, trying to reassure him. But her pain was etched clearly on her face.

Protective need surged inside him. He put the sarong under her foot. Using the ends, he wiped away the blood, trying to get a clear picture of the wound. A flash of pearly white bone could be clearly seen before blood spurted out, occluding the area.

Her foot needed more than a sticky plaster. His heart pounded and his stomach turned over, the familiar tension and fear jetting up inside him. He started to wrap her foot tightly to staunch the bleeding, his arm shaking with each wind of the sarong.

You can use a jig-saw without shaking. He gritted his teeth and kept rolling, the action clumsy.

Wood is replaceable if I make a mistake.

'How does it look?' Sarah stared at the sarong.

'Your foot needs stitching.' The bald words came out drenched with hatred for his dysfunctional body.

She put her head in her hands and her shoulders sagged, all her usual doggedness and determination flowing out of her.

She needs a doctor who isn't going to stuff up.

Her dejection tore at him. She needed pain relief, stitches and crutches, and possibly a tetanus shot.

He reached out and touched the back of her head, wanting to give comfort, her hair silky against his hand.

Her voice shook. 'It's over two hours to Cairns.'

And the road from here was rough and corrugated. She needed him. Needed him to be the doctor.

His hand shook at the thought. This time she wouldn't be standing next to him to bail him out. Acid burned his stomach. The arguments in his head went round and round.

This is Sarah.

He had to do this. He couldn't refuse her.

He swung into action. 'Sam, you're doing a great job but I need you to be my legs again.' He pointed to the food bag. 'Open it up and in the black netting at the top you'll find my car keys.'

'And I press the button to unlock the door?'

Ryan nodded. 'Yes, but press the smaller button to unlock the boot and then bring Mum's medical bag over to the picnic table on the grass just before the sand starts.' He pointed in the general direction.

'OK.' Sam's chest puffed out with the responsibility and he ran back to the bag.

He turned to Sarah and formed a question. He had no right to assume and she had the right to refuse the ministrations of a tremor-torn doctor. 'Sarah, are you OK with me stitching your foot?'

She placed her hand on his arm. 'I thought you'd never offer.'

'I can't guarantee you a neat scar.' He hated speaking the words, admitting the weakness.

'The sole of my foot and I are just thankful you're here before I lose any more blood.' She tried to smile but the shock had started to sap her of energy.

He didn't want to stitch on the sand, he needed to find the cleanest area he could. 'Do you think you can stand on one foot and hop a hundred metres, using me for some support?'

She looked up at him, resignation on her face. 'I guess I'm going to have to unless I want stonewashed sutures and a raging infection.'

She pushed up onto her knees and bent her good leg.

Ryan put his weight on his stick and leaned forward. Somehow he managed to help Sarah up onto her uninjured leg without them both falling in a heap. In small bursts of hopping she managed to get to the grass where she collapsed onto the bench seat attached to the picnic table.

'I've got the bag, Ryan.' Sam proudly put it on the table and handed Ryan his keys.

Ryan squeezed his shoulder. 'Well done, mate. Now, I need you to sit next to Mum and hold her hand because I'm going to fix her foot.'

Sam dutifully sat next to Sarah.

Ryan opened Sarah's bag and peered in.

'The xylocaine is in the black plastic box and the silk packs are in the zippered section.' Sarah swung her leg up onto the bench. 'There's also a dressing pack and a blue sheet and the syringes—'

Ryan turned to look at her, raising his brows. 'I believe you're the patient, Sarah, so sit back and leave it to me.'

'I was only trying to help.' Pain and anxiety lined her face.

'Yeah, Mum. Ryan knows what he's doing. He's really organised at the house and he says you have to get everything laid out and ready before you even start, don't you, Ryan?'

He smiled at the unexpected support. 'That's right.

But Mum's a bit upset so you tell her a joke while I give her an injection to take the pain away.'

He picked up the glass ampoule of local anaesthetic. Breathing deeply, he closed his eyes and visualised the procedure that was technically so straightforward a medical student could have attempted it. But he didn't want to just attempt it. He needed to do it and do it well. His signature would be on Sarah's foot for ever.

Damn it, it was going to be a neat job with tiny stitches.

He snapped off the top of the ampoule and inserted the needle into the tiny hole. He drew up the clear fluid deftly and capped the lid.

Straddling the end of the bench, he positioned her foot between his legs. He carefully unwrapped the sarong and cleaned her foot with normal saline, washing away the sand. Then he swabbed the skin with alcohol swabs. 'OK, needle time. Sam, hold your mum's hand.' He stared at Sarah. 'This will sting a bit.'

She bit her lip and nodded.

He slid the needle into her foot at a shallow angle, infiltrating the area with the numbing liquid. 'Sam, you tell me when five minutes have gone past.'

'OK, Ryan.'

He opened the dressing pack, the suture material, the Betadine and looked at the awful plastic forceps that never worked well even when his arm didn't shake. Hell. They weren't designed for suturing and would slip on the needle.

Fine-pointed vice grips. 'Sam, can you head back to my car and bring my tool kit and the bottle of methylated spirits?'

Sam jumped up and caught the keys Ryan tossed him. 'I'll be quick.' He ran toward to car.

Ryan put his hand on Sarah's leg. 'He's a sensational kid, Sarah.'

Her love for Sam shone on her face. 'He is.' Suddenly tears fell down her cheek and she quickly wiped them away. 'I feel so foolish. Why am I crying? I've only cut my foot and…'

He picked up her hands and squeezed them, trying to reassure her. 'It's the shock, and it's not just a cut— it's a mighty deep gash. I can see the bone.'

A shudder ran through her. 'I'm glad you're here.' She sounded young and vulnerable, not the usual in-control woman he knew.

He kissed her hand, trying to reassure her.

Sam returned with the requested goods. 'What do you need this for?'

Ryan picked up the vice grips from the tool kit and poured the methylated spirits over them to sterilise the metal. 'I'll use these to control the needle as I stitch.'

'Cool!'

'Can you feel this?' He pressed the point of a needle against Sarah's foot.

'Nope, nothing.'

'Great, I can start.' His voice sounded a lot more certain than he felt. First he irrigated the wound, flushing out any dirt or glass. *That's the easy bit.*

Using one pair of the dreaded plastic forceps and the vice grips, he started to stitch the deepest layer of muscle, the one closest to the bone. The curved needle slid through the tissue and the grips held it firmly.

He felt the tremble start at his elbow.

You're trying too hard. Relax. Loosen your grip on the pliers.

He breathed out and softened his grip. The tremor faded.

He glanced up and saw in Sarah's eyes her total belief in his ability. Sam's expression radiated complete confidence.

For the first time since his accident he started to believe. Pushing the needle through the skin again, he continued. He dropped the suture.

He picked it up.

The ends of the plastic forceps missed.

He tried again.

Every hint of a tremor he stalled by concentrating on Sarah and Sam's belief in him.

Unconsciously, he found a rhythm as he pushed and pulled the needle through the muscle, capably alternating between the pliers and the plastic forceps.

Threads of excitement wove together deep inside him as he brought the layers of damaged tissue back into alignment. He grinned. God, it felt good.

He snipped the fine silk that he'd used to close the layer of skin. A row of tiny black stiches was the only hint of the jagged damage the glass had caused.

Sarah moved her foot so she could see. 'Oh, Ryan, that's so neat.'

He grinned like a kid. 'Told you I was known for neat stitches.'

She gave him a tired smile. 'Thank you.'

'My pleasure.' A feeling of lightness, unlike anything he'd experienced, filled him.

He put on a non-stick dressing to protect the area and

then bandaged her foot. 'Right, I'll bring the car over here and we'll get you home and started on antibiotics. You'll be non-weight-bearing for at least a week.'

A horrified expression crossed her face. 'A week! I can't sit around with my foot up for a week.'

'Sorry, doctor's orders.' He started wrapping up all the rubbish.

'Ryan, if I'm non-weight-bearing then Yakkaburra needs a doctor.' Sarah's voice sounded behind him.

His hands stilled on the rolled-up dressing pack. 'I guess it does.' He turned slowly back to face her.

'Will you be that doctor?' Her expression was neutral, as if she expected nothing from him at all but thought it politic to ask him first.

He waited for his chest to tighten. For his stomach to clench, for the abject fear that usually swamped him when he thought of work.

Nothing.

A kernel of anticipation expanded inside him. *Working with patients again.* A thrill replaced the terror that had become so much a part of him.

It suddenly felt right.

It was time to back to being a doctor and Yakkaburra was a good place to start. 'Yes, I'd be happy to help.'

CHAPTER EIGHT

'HAZEL to see you, Ryan.' Jenny ushered the elderly lady into the office and mouthed over her head, 'Last patient.'

Ryan stood and came around the desk to guide Hazel into the chair.

Brilliant blue eyes sparkled from a wizened face as she lowered herself into the chair. She tapped her cane against his. 'Nice-looking stick, son. Although the handle's a bit plain.'

A belly laugh rumbled up and out of Ryan. 'An eight-year-old told me the same thing.'

'Well, I'm eighty so listen to the number eight—we know things.' She rested back in the seat. 'So what happened to you?'

Ryan was getting used to the question. This week he reckoned half the patients had come to interview him rather than the other way around. At first he'd resisted talking about his leg but then he'd realised most people had a genuine concern rather than the 'gawk' factor.

He pulled up a chair and sat down next to her. 'I came off second best when a four-wheel-drive ploughed into me.'

She nodded slowly, as if absorbing that information. She tilted her head to one side. 'You look like Edna.'

Surprise filled him. 'You knew my grandmother?'

'And you, dear.' She extended her hand. 'Hazel Papadopoulos. You used to come to visit me when you were little and we'd cook biscuits and make cakes.'

A memory stirred—the sweet spice of cinnamon, the stickiness of glacé fruit, licking the beaters, his tongue wrapping around the silver edges, not wanting to miss a drop. 'Mrs Pap?' He clasped her hand, her dry paper-thin skin cool against his palm.

She smiled. 'That's right. It was a long time ago.'

He looked at this kind old lady, the memories of times spent in her fragrant kitchen now stronger. Cooking and love. 'Why did I stop coming?'

'My Peter went off to boarding school and I think you thought at twelve you were too big to come and spend time with your mate's grandmother when he wasn't there.' She patted his knee. 'Then you became a teenager and you thought the world was against you.'

'The town was.' The hurt he thought he'd disengaged from surged forward.

She shook her head with the wisdom of the aged. 'No, it wasn't. The ignorant ones talk the loudest and matter the least, but when you're young you can't see that.'

She clicked her tongue. 'People didn't understand that your mum was sick, and it's too easy to criticise what you don't understand.' She took in a deep breath. 'Your mother's illness broke your grandmother's heart. But she loved you dearly and tried her best to protect you from the narrow-minded bigots.'

She wrung her hands, her eyes misting. 'She was so

proud of you. She knew you had to leave Yakkaburra to find yourself and now look at you—you're a fine doctor, so everyone in town tells me. You have her spirit.'

His throat tightened at Hazel's words, images and memories pounding at him from all sides. All week he'd met patients who talked to him about his grandmother, all of them vocal in their respect and admiration for her.

See the town through adult eyes. Sarah's lilting voice played across his mind.

He thought about his weeks in Yakkaburra. The warm welcome, his acceptance back into town life, even though he'd tried to resist it. The times the town had surprised him.

Something shifted inside him. Perhaps it was the adolescent scales falling away from his eyes. But suddenly he saw Yakkaburra as it really was—a small town with hard-working people, most of whom wished their neighbours well and supported each other through good times and bad.

'Thank you, Mrs Pap. I think you've just done more for me than an analyst could ever do. Now, what can I do for you?'

She beamed at him. 'Well, I'd like a new heart and new legs, dear, but I'll settle for another prescription of those heart tablets Sarah put me on.'

Half an hour later Ryan pulled into Sarah's driveway, dodging Sam's bike and basketball, which lay in the drive. Usually Sam was waiting for him and they played a bit of 'stationary shoot-out,' tossing baskets from a particular part of the 'court'. Ryan was getting pretty good on the one-handed toss.

He grabbed his medical bag and a large bunch of bright red anthuriums, and headed up the path to the front door. His leg burned and dragged. His arm ached. Tiredness clung to him.

And he loved it, embracing all of it—the legacy of an amazing, challenging and stimulating seven days working back in medicine. He'd always thought clinic work would exacerbate his loss of surgery. Instead, he'd realised it eased it.

He opened the door and was immediately struck by the unusual quietness. No music or TV. 'Hello, it's me.' He stepped inside.

He heard the thud of Sarah's crutches before he saw her. She rounded the corner from the kitchen wearing a short skirt that seemed to flare out with each step she took, exposing her toned, tanned legs. Hinting at what lay above the hemline.

Familiar heat and visceral craving pounded through him.

She looked up and smiled. 'Hi.'

A sense of lightness tagged the initial heat. For the past week he'd found himself looking forward to the end of the day, knowing he'd be visiting Sarah and Sam as soon as his clinic day was over. He'd drop in and give her a clinic handover, often culminating in a healthy discussion on treatment options for some trickier cases.

It isn't always, 'If in doubt, cut it out,' Sarah had teased him. General practice's diversity threw up different challenges for him and he loved the mental gymnastics involved. Especially with Sarah.

Sometimes he stayed for dinner; sometimes he brought dinner with him. Other nights he borrowed Sam for an hour or so to work on the house. After Sam went home to bed he'd continue on his own. Who'd have thought restoring his grandmother's house would be so relaxing?

'No Sam tonight?'

She shook her head. 'Mum and Dad kidnapped him for the night, bribing him with pizza, a movie and the promise of being a plumber's mate.' She gave him a direct look. 'They said they hadn't seen much of him lately.'

Ryan cheerfully admitted to monopolising Sam's time. 'Trying to compete against my renovations with plumbing, are they?' He harrumphed in mock derision. 'No power tools in plumbing.'

She raised her brows, her lips, curving upwards into a devilish grin. 'You might be outdone. Dad's got a mate with a back-hoe.'

He laughed, loving the camaraderie they shared. He'd never experienced that with any other woman.

She looked toward his bag, her face glowing with excitement. 'Did you bring it?'

'Bring what?' He deliberately acted obtuse. How could he forget today? Sarah had been counting down the days until her stitches could be removed and had messaged him twice at work to remind him.

She playfully swung a crutch at him. 'Hey, no stitch-cutter, no prawn salad.'

He put his hands up, pretending to defend himself. 'I brought the stitch-cutter already.'

She plonked herself on the couch. Flashes of skin, lace and skirt intermingled as she lifted her foot up onto the coffee-table. 'Let's do it.'

Stars exploded in his head. 'Right.' He cleared his throat. 'Operation stitch removal coming up.'

Five minutes later, a transparent, waterproof dressing was the only evidence left of the injury. 'You can get rid of the crutches now but don't overdo things.'

Her eyes twinkled at him. 'As if I would.'

He shook his head. 'I virtually had to tie you to the bed to get you to stay off your foot this long.'

Desire flared in her eyes and she nibbled her bottom lip.

Lust, hot and base, thudded through him and he groaned internally at his poor choice of words.

And the image they generated.

As each day passed, the more time they spent together, the harder it became for him not to act on the electrically charged attraction that existed between them. He wanted her in his arms, her body melded to his.

But Sarah had said, "I guess it hovers." No matter how hard he found it, and he found it excruciatingly tough, he had to respect her wishes.

Sarah's heart pounded against her ribs. Ryan's face projected a look of unadulterated hunger. And it wasn't for prawns. He wanted her.

With sudden clarity she realised that since the night at the beach he'd stopped hiding his desire for her. He was always discreet when Sam was around, and Sam had pretty much been with them this week, so she'd missed the full significance. Until now.

And tonight Sam was out.

Ryan's hands grasped hers and he hauled her to her feet, his breath caressing her face. 'I brought you some celebratory flowers.'

'Thank you.' Her heart soared at his thoughtfulness. 'I've got some celebratory champagne.'

He stepped in close until the space between them was so minute she could almost feel his length pressing on hers. His dark eyes looked into her soul. 'Guess we should celebrate then.' His low voice rumbled around her.

He wants you. Take him, he's yours tonight.

She steeled herself against the tempting voice. *What about Sam? What about tomorrow?*

The voice wouldn't be silenced. *Sam isn't here. Tomorrow will bring regrets either way.*

Oh, how she knew that. Tomorrow was never reliable. Her life with David had taught her that.

A choice lay before her.

She reached up and placed her palm flat against his cheek, his end-of-day stubble gloriously rough against her skin. 'I don't want to let it hover any more. Let's just go with the flow and see where it takes us. No expectations.'

His sable eyes explored her face, searching for any uncertainty on her part as his finger traced her cheekbone with a butterfly touch. 'Are you sure?'

Tiny shots of tingling sensation danced along her cheek. She moved her head, the slightest nod forward. *Yes, I really want this.*

His lips swept across hers in a kiss so gentle, so tender that a part of her cried out in sweet pain. *Treasured.* But she wouldn't let her mind go there.

Here and now was all that mattered. Nothing else could be depended on.

Slowly the pressure of his lips changed, the kiss deepened. Concentrated desire, potent and intoxicating, poured through her all the way down to her toes. She melted against him, never wanting it to stop.

He raised his head, his breathing ragged. 'I wish I could swing you into my arms and carry you to bed.'

She grabbed his hand and smiled. 'Let's limp there together.'

He laughed, a sound of pure elation. 'I bet I can limp faster than you.'

They lurched and laughed the short distance to her bedroom and fell on the bed together. Laughter immediately transformed into groans of longing, the release of weeks of stifled yearning and aching awareness.

She reached for his shirt, her fingers trembling with need, unable to force the buttons through the holes quickly enough. She moaned in frustration.

His wicked chuckle teased her. 'Hey, I'm the one with the tremors.' He deftly pulled the shirt over his head and pulled her close.

She ran her hands along his chest, feeling the contours of his muscles, the small valleys between the tight bands. Here and now, this chest, his skin, it all belonged to her. She memorised the sight, the feel of him under her hand, the musky scent of his skin and the taste of him, her tongue absorbing and imprinting at the same time.

His hand ran up her leg, firing her already stoked need to fever pitch. His hand closed on the curve of her behind, kneading the skin, his fingers teasingly close to the incredibly sensitive spot at the top of her thighs.

Sparks of silver light flashed in front of her eyes and she arched toward him. Her body acted on instinct, freed by her decision, responding to his touch demanding more, giving more.

His legs wrapped around hers, skin on skin, heat on wondrous heat.

She dropped her hand onto his leg.

His muscles contracted, rigid with tension, and he tried to move her hand to his other leg.

'Shh.' Her mouth covered his as her fingers explored the thickened scars, the concave grafts, the rough skin and the smooth.

He slowly relaxed into her kiss.

Keeping one hand on his face, she laid her lips on his leg, trailing kisses along the scars. Kisses of acceptance, and healing, slowly morphing into hot, demanding kisses.

He pulled her into his arms, holding her tight and close, her chest pressed hard against his. His eyes swirled with myriad emotions too hard to read before he buried his face into her neck.

She held him. For a brief moment all was still.

Then her fingers dug into his hair, silky strands soft against her palm.

His tongue found her ear.

Instantly, they moved together, reaching for each other, shedding clothes, trying to stay connected amid fumblings and tangles, laughter and desperate longing.

He hauled off her T-shirt and suddenly stilled. Wonder mixed with unashamed lust as he stared at her breasts, the lace of the bra barely concealing what lay beneath.

She squashed the tiny flare of doubt that made her want to reach for her shirt and cover herself. These breasts had worked—she'd fed a baby. But Ryan's hunger for her stalled that thought. She sat back, accepting his admiring gaze.

He laid his thumb against the lace and with a

feather-like touch arced it back and forth, barely grazing skin and lace.

Every nerve ending roared into overdrive, competing to respond, showering her with wave upon wave of sensation. Sheer, aching pleasure.

'My turn now.' With one deft flick he released her bra and her breasts tumbled into his hands. He brought his mouth down to them.

Everything around her faded to nothing. All that existed was his mouth on her breast, his tongue on her nipple and the ribbons of liquid sensation that flowed into the very heart of her.

She pulled at him, her hands kneading the muscles of his back, wanting to feel all of him, desperate for release yet needing to make this wondrous feeling, this connection, last for ever.

'You're so beautiful.' Ryan's husky voice whispered against her ear as his hand moved slowly down her belly, creating a trail of sweet, endless torment.

She bucked toward him as his fingers found their target. Overwhelming need crashed against her. Her belly tightened, her whole body throbbed as she flung her head back on the bed.

'Can't wait.' The words came out on shallow gasps as her fingers gripped his head.

He swallowed her cry of release with his mouth, giving and taking simultaneously. With whispered words, he entered her and slowly rebuilt her heat until she teetered on the precipice again.

This time they tumbled together, soaring out into the darkness, connected in the moment. Unified. Two bodies as one.

* * *

She lay with his arms around her, his leg resting between hers, her back curved into his chest and belly. Cocooned.

'That was amazing.' His breath tickled her cheek.

She snuggled against him. 'It was.'

His hand cupped her breast. 'So, exactly *when* is Sam due home?'

She laughed and rolled over to face him. 'Tomorrow afternoon.'

'So that gives us…' he dropped a kiss on her nose '…all night.' He kissed her cheek. 'And part of tomorrow.' He kissed her neck. 'I'll cook you breakfast before work…' His lips trailed along her collar-bone.

Whirls of colour pushed at her concentration as his kisses rained down on her skin. 'I thought you couldn't cook.'

His fingers tickled her under her ribs. 'Cheeky. Keep that up and I'll put mango on the menu.'

Her laughter tumbled from her lips. Elation and joy cascaded like a waterfall, rushing through the crevices inside her, releasing an overwhelming sense of belonging and security. *He's staying for breakfast.* She wanted to squeal with happiness.

Don't get used to it. It never lasts. A niggle of reality tried to take hold. Remember, no expectations.

She pressed her body against his, feeling all of him against her, and kissed him long and hard, slamming the door shut on the voice.

'Coffee?'

Sarah glanced up from the medical report she was writing and a familiar rush of heat whirled inside her.

Ryan stood smiling, leaning casually against his cane and completely filling the doorway of her office.

All evidence of the city surgeon had faded. They'd been working together for a month. Sharing a bed when Sam was at his grandparents', sharing meals most nights. Over that time his wardrobe had slowly changed, becoming more casual. Instead of long black business trousers that hid his scars, beige cargo shorts now hung off his hips, exposing his tanned legs and the legacy of the accident.

But even though he'd relaxed a lot, today's shirt was off the chart, sunglasses worthy, and it screamed Far North Queensland 'holiday-maker'.

It was so *not* Ryan. 'Where on earth did you get that shirt?'

He grinned. 'Jim brought it back from Port Douglas. He said I needed to embrace the region now I'm back, and life was too short to only wear black and white.'

She laughed. 'And he's got a follow-up appointment with you this afternoon.'

He looked sheepish. 'Yeah, so I thought I'd better wear it. Then I can bury it in the back of the wardrobe.'

Her heart sang. Ryan had embraced general practice, caring for his patients as real people, not just a sore left leg or upper quadrant pain. The shirt was testament to that.

She stood up and walked over to him, her arms snaking around his waist. 'You're just a big softie, aren't you?'

He kissed her forehead. 'I have to admit this town and the people are growing on me.'

He might stay. Hope kicked her hard.

And he might not. She dropped her arms and stepped back. 'So where's this coffee you promised me?'

The intercom buzzed. 'Sarah, Ryan.' Jenny's voice crackled. 'Ava Burton is vomiting in the treatment room, with a temp of forty and complaining of stomach pains.'

'Coming now.' Their voices merged.

Ryan frowned as he started to walk down the corridor. 'I saw Ava a week ago. She had vague symptoms of a rumbling appendix and with kids it's just as likely to settle. But I told her mother to bring her back the moment anything changed.'

'Looks like it just did.' Sarah walked into the treatment room to see Jenny stroking a young girl's forehead. Ten-year-old Ava lay curled up on the examination table, her skin sallow and sunken. 'I'll put up the IV.'

Ryan bent down close to the little girl. 'Not feeling so good, Ava?'

'My tummy hurts really bad, Dr Ryan.' A couple of tears trailed down her face. 'Where's Mummy?'

'Mum's on her way, sweetie.' Jenny handed the observation chart to Ryan. 'School brought her over.'

'Ava, I have to put a needle in your arm. It will sting a little but then we can give you something to stop the vomiting.' Sarah wiped the girl's skin with the alcohol swab.

'OK, I guess.'

Her frightened voice tugged at Sarah.

Ryan flicked through the chart, his frown deepening. 'When did you last have something to eat or drink, Ava?'

'I didn't eat any breakfast and I only drank water this morning.'

Ryan bobbed down so he was at eye level with Ava. 'I need to press your tummy so I can see if your pesky appendix is playing up.'

The girl's face crumpled, everything now overwhelming her. 'Will it hurt?'

'I'll be as gentle as I can.' His large hand gently palpated the girl's lower abdomen.

Ava flinched and gripped Jenny's hand.

'You've been really brave, Ava, thank you.' He stepped away from the examination table and inclined his head to Sarah who met him at the desk.

'Guarding and tenderness in the right iliac fossa?' Sarah tried to read both Ava and Ryan.

He nodded. 'She needs surgery.'

'Ask Jenny to ring the ambulance and notify Cairns Base that—'

'I want to do the surgery.'

Surprise froze her brain. She shifted mental gears. 'Oh, OK, so you'll go to Cairns with her.' Her mind raced ahead. 'Right, ring Phillip Leighton and he can arrange admitting rights and book a theatre for you.'

'No, you don't understand. I want to do the surgery here.'

'But we don't have a laparoscope.' The words blurted out quickly.

Ryan folded his arms. 'Ava doesn't need her appendix rupturing. Right now we have a contained situation but in three hours she might have peritonitis. I'll do a tiny incision.' He put his hand on her arm. 'Will you do the anaesthetic?'

Everything he said made perfect sense. They'd coped with Jim and compared to that this was very straightforward. 'Of course.'

He clapped his hands together loudly, the surgeon in full organising mode. 'Jenny, get me a set of consent forms, tell me the moment Ava's mother arrives and ring Karen and tell her we need her to scout.' He turned back to Sarah. 'You organise the anaesthetic. Jenny and I will bring Ava into Theatre as soon as her mother has arrived and signed the forms.'

Twenty minutes later, Sarah noted Ava's stable pulse rate and adjusted the mild anaesthetic.

'The diathermy's been serviced and I've checked it twice,' Karen commented, as she added the suture material to the sterile tray.

'Great. Thanks.' Ryan gave it a test run anyway.

Ryan's dark eyes caught Sarah's gaze over the sterile drape, his brows rising in question.

She nodded. 'All set my end.'

'Excellent.' He put out his gloved hand to Jenny. 'Scalpel.'

A spark of pleasure and pride shot through her. He'd found his way. He was back in surgery where he belonged.

Sarah followed every movement. Ryan's steady hands incised the skin, controlled the bleeding, located the appendix, using as small a space as possible, and deftly tied off the stump. Sheer bliss expanded inside her at his technique. He hadn't faltered once.

His neat stitching meant Ava could wear a bikini as a teenager and no one would be any the wiser that she'd parted company with her appendix.

Sarah reversed the anaesthetic and with Karen wheeled Ava into Recovery. 'She's stable so buzz me if you have any concerns. I've written up IV and antibiotic orders to cover the night.'

'Thanks, Sarah.' Karen wrapped the blood-pressure cuff around Ava's arm and started post-op observations.

Sarah found Ryan in the staffroom, writing up the history. She put her hands on his shoulders. 'You were great.'

He swivelled around to face her. 'It felt so damn good.'

Somehow he looked different. In the last few weeks he'd smiled and laughed more and more, so it wasn't the broad grin or the sexy dimple in his cheek.

Realisation shook her down to her toes. His eyes. His glorious eyes that went from midnight black to sparkling opal black were no longer haunted by shadows.

She swallowed against the sudden lump in her throat. The tortured man had found his way back, right here in Yakkaburra.

'Sit.' He pulled out a chair, his entire body dancing with animation. 'I want to run something past you.'

His total enthusiasm was contagious. 'Tell me,' she said.

'I want to open the hospital's theatre once a week for surgery.'

Astonishment jolted her. 'What sort of surgery?'

'Carpel tunnel, gastroscopies, biopsies, things like that. But it would also give us the facility to use it for situations like today.'

Her mind ran through all the options. 'What about an anaesthetist? I'm a GP, Ryan.'

'We're not talking trauma surgery. You were brilliant today but you can add to that with some training in Cairns.'

Excitement bubbled inside her but she tried to stay on top of it and ask the necessary questions. 'We'd need extra funding for equipment. The powers that be are closing country hospitals, not opening them.'

'True, but often it's because they can't get surgeons.'

He pushed some papers toward her. 'I've been thinking about this for a couple of weeks. This is an application for more funding. Would you support it?'

Would she support it? It would mean Yakkaburra wouldn't be as dependent on Innisfail and Cairns. It would mean patients didn't have to travel long distances for straightforward procedures.

'Of course I'll support it.'

His eyes sparkled. 'Sensational.'

Hope gurgled up inside her. This must mean Ryan was planning on staying in Yakkaburra.

Not necessarily. Nothing is permanent.

True, but right now he was here and for once in her life she was being selfish and taking what was on offer. No strings attached. Just going with the flow, like they'd agreed.

Surely there was no harm in that.

CHAPTER NINE

THE town hall clock struck one. 'Yikes, listen to the time.' Sarah didn't realise how much she depended on the loudness of that clock to drive her day until it roused her from her pathology reports.

'Sarah, it's time to go.' Jenny's cheery voice burst into the room from the intercom.

'Thanks. I'm on my way.' She loved the big clock but having Jenny as back-up helped. This afternoon was too important to miss.

She grabbed her bag, and headed next door to the hospital to find Ryan. She heard his deep melodic voice before she saw him and felt the now familiar quiver of longing. She'd wondered if that reaction might have lessened since they'd made love. But, if anything, it had intensified.

'Karen, page me if John Ricardo's condition changes. Keep an eye on the drain tube. He's stable at the moment but that gall bladder was really filthy.'

'Will do, Ryan.' Karen added the volume of the new IV bag to the pink fluid balance chart.

Sarah stood by the door, watching him at work,

polite, professional and caring. She could have watched him all day.

He turned, caught sight of her and smiled, his face softened by the cheeky dimple in his cheek and dancing eyes. 'I'm almost done, promise.'

She nodded, not remotely stressed. When Ryan committed to do something, he followed through.

He did a final check on Mr Ricardo's dressing, drain tube and urine output. 'I'll be back around three but call me if you need me.'

Karen rolled her eyes. 'Just go already.'

He laughed and walked away, his gait much improved, less jerky than it had been, and he was beside Sarah in a moment. 'Who's driving?'

'You. My car's being serviced.' She joined his quicker pace out toward the car park, suddenly struck by the conversation. They sounded like a couple. *No way. Don't think like that.*

He checked his watch. 'We'll make it, won't we?'

A cocoon of warmth spun inside her at his concern. 'We'll make it easily.'

Ten minutes later the strong smell of chlorine stung Sarah's nostrils as she pushed through the Yakkaburra Public Pool's turnstile. She stepped onto the lawn, almost deafened by the roar of three hundred school kids cheering for their teams. Banners waved in the breeze, blocks of colour moved as one as the kids dressed in the colours of their schools chanted their teams home. The pool water churned white with the enthusiasm and competitiveness of the swimmers.

Ryan's hand touched her elbow. 'Wow, I had no

idea the regional swimming competition would be this big an event.'

She laughed. 'How could you not know? It's all Sam's spoken about for a week.'

He looked abashed. 'True. So where do we sit?'

She pointed to the opposite side of the pool from the kids. 'Over there will give us a good view.'

She flicked out the picnic rug and sat down, nodding and smiling to other parents. Unfortunately her own parents had to go to a funeral in Cairns and would miss Sam's debut swimming race. Sam had asked Ryan if he'd like to come.

She knew he'd reorganised his day to accommodate the race and the gesture touched her. Over the weeks she'd watched a special bond build between her son and this man. He treated Sam as a person with an opinion rather than a child.

Perhaps it had something to do with Ryan growing up with an absent father, although she suspected it was more to do with the impact of his university mentor. Whatever the reason, she appreciated the effort. It had come at a good time for Sam.

He'd make a great father.

The insistent inner voice had started getting bold. She extinguished it. She'd had her one shot at marriage. Sam would survive with grandfathers and mentors.

Ryan lowered himself down next to her a few minutes later, having been waylaid chatting to some people. He was so much more at ease with the town since he'd started working. Her heart picked up as his leg brushed hers.

'How many races until the big backstroke event?' Ryan scanned the crowd, trying to find Sam.

'He said it would start around one-thirty.'

Ryan suddenly pressed down on his stick and stood up, waving his arm straight out over his head, finishing with a thumbs-up sign. 'Sam's over there, lining up behind the other starters.' He hauled her to her feet. 'See.'

She jumped up and down, trying to see over the crowd. 'Where?'

He grinned wickedly. 'You're such a shortie.'

She gave him a mock push but his arm caught her around her waist and swung her into his solid chest.

He murmured, 'Short and amazingly gorgeous.' Almost as quickly as he'd pulled her to him he let her go, the action short, powerful and discreet.

Happiness hummed through her at his touch. She peered around the group in front of her. 'I see him. He's getting into the pool for the start.'

'We worked on his start.'

Astonished, she turned to face him. 'Really? When?'

A sheepish expression crossed his face. 'Last week, when you were running your heart health information evening. He comes off the wall well and can do a pretty mean tumble-turn.'

'This is primary school sport, Ryan.'

He stiffened slightly. 'And Sam wants to do his personal best. I just gave him some tips.'

For a second she glimpsed the small boy who'd struggled through childhood. He didn't want her son to have the same battles. She squeezed his arm, warmth filling her. 'Thanks.'

Sam brought his small but sturdy legs up under his chin as his hands gripped the silver starting bar.

The starting gun fired.

Sarah held her breath.

The water churned as six eight-year-old boys powered up their lanes, their arms and legs thrashing the water, occasionally colliding with the ropes. Sam was level with two other boys as they came to the turn.

Sam flipped back in an arc, his legs pushing off the wall as he spun back onto his back.

'A perfect turn.' Sarah clapped her hands.

Sam shot in front of the other two boys and in a steady, determined rhythm he ploughed through the water.

Yakkaburra Primary School screamed and roared as Sam moved ahead.

Ryan cupped his hands to his mouth. 'Go, Sam.'

Sarah's heart pounded fast and hard and she almost couldn't look.

The boy from Tully caught up.

The noise doubled.

Sarah started to jump up and down, unable to restrain her excitement any longer.

Sam touched the wall first.

Sarah squealed with delight.

'Yes!' Ryan's arm shot straight into the air.

Pride, excitement, laughter and wonder played across his face.

He pulled her into his arms, his eyes sparkling. 'He did it!'

'I know, I can't believe it, I could hardly look.'

'He swam the perfect race.' Ryan's mouth swept lightly across her lips. A kiss of joy, a kiss of shared experiences, all bundled together with a sense of belonging.

The kiss travelled through her, touching places never visited before. Releasing a sense of connection, of pure happiness unconnected with desire. Releasing love.

She loved him.

Oh, God no.

She couldn't love him. This was a fling while he got back on his feet. She'd wanted to help him but not love him. She didn't want to love anyone again. Didn't want to be hurt again.

But it was too late.

She loved this complicated and caring man. Part lover, part friend and part mentor to her son. She loved the whole man.

And that terrified her. Left her vulnerable.

A series of rapid beeps broke through her haze.

Ryan sighed. 'Oh, no. Mr Ricardo must have deteriorated. I'll see Sam on my way out.' He squeezed her hand. 'Catch you later.'

She watched him move through the crowd, saw him high-five Sam and give his shoulder a tight squeeze. A thought so clear rocked her hard and she almost swayed.

This time she'd fallen in love with a good man. This time she'd got it right.

And he hadn't mentioned Melbourne in a long time. Just lately he'd seemed content working and renovating and spending time with herself and Sam. He'd started operating again.

He had a house and a life in Yakkaburra.

She hugged herself tight with the thought.

Ryan rang the hospital as he walked to the car.

Karen's anxious voice came down the line. 'It's not

Mr Ricardo. There's been a motorbike accident on the Turpin Road. Jack requested your back-up.'

'On my way.' He dropped the phone onto the front seat of the car and gunned it out of the car park. He heard the sirens before he saw the accident. The police, already in attendance, had cordoned off the area with bright yellow tape.

He strode toward Sergeant Jack, who was bent over a body.

Jack looked up, his usually taciturn expression lanced with distress. 'The ambulance is on its way. Thank goodness you're here, Ryan, it's Tim Nguyen.'

Tim lay sprawled on the road, eerily still, his leathers clinging to limbs that contorted at rakish angles.

Images of a gregarious eighteen-year-old, preparing to head off to uni in a few months played out in vivid Technicolor in Ryan's brain, along with pictures of his proud parents thrilled that their first-generation Australian son was trail-blazing for the family.

His stomach dropped, nausea filling him. Vivid flashes of his own accident streamed through his mind. He threw himself into action, knowing he had no time to waste.

He checked the unconscious youth's airway. It was clear but he was breathing in shallow, rapid breaths. Using the shears from Jack's kit, he cut the leather and clothes until he could visualize Tim's chest.

He placed his hands on his ribcage. The chest moved in on inspiration and out on expiration. Flail chest. He moved his hands further down the torso. Guarded abdomen. Internal bleeding.

Damn it to hell. 'He's got a massive fight on his

hands, Jack. Ring the air ambulance and then get Sarah on the phone. She'll have to tell his parents.'

'Will do, Ryan.' Jack ran back to his vehicle.

The screaming sirens got closer and suddenly stopped. The ambos ran quickly toward him with their gear.

Ryan looked up. 'Good to see you, fellas. Mike, he's bleeding so get two lines of Hartmann's going. Greg, we need to stabilise his neck and logroll him onto the scoop stretcher,' Ryan instructed. 'Then I'll tube him to maintain his airway.'

The experienced paramedics nodded and went into action. Greg slid the neck brace in place while Ryan removed Tim's helmet, keeping everything as smooth and steady as possible.

'On my count we'll roll.' Ryan controlled the upper part of Tim's body while Greg controlled the legs.

Skilfully, the two men positioned the critically ill Tim on the stretcher.

Mike immediately attached the skin dots to Tim's chest and started up the portable cardiac monitor.

Ryan flicked open the laryngoscope, inserting it into Tim's mouth, and quickly located the vocal cords. He slid the ET tube into place and Greg promptly attached the air viva and commenced bagging Tim for extra oxygen.

'BP's pretty low, Ryan.' Mike pulled the stethoscope out of his ears.

'Run the IV full blast.' Ryan continued to examine Tim. 'Fractured clavicle, fractured ribs, fractured pelvis— he's a bloody mess. Where the hell is that helicopter?'

'Should be here soon.' Greg automatically scanned the sky.

The portable cardiac monitor's steady rhythm

changed. Incessant beeping, unrelenting. 'He's arrested!' Mike immediately started CPR.

'We're giving him circulating volume but he's got to be bleeding into his belly.' Ryan reached for adrenaline, snapped the top off the ampoule and drew up one milligram. He plunged the heart-starting drug into the rubber bung of the IV tube.

He charged the defibrillator. 'Stand clear.' He pressed the button, shocking Tim's heart, praying for him to respond.

'Sinus rhythm.' Greg's worried voice held a tinge of triumph.

Ryan sighed. 'Yeah, but for how long?' Straining his ears, he willed the helicopter to arrive to give Tim a fighting chance of survival.

Ryan stepped out of the state-of-the-art theatre in Cairns Base Hospital, leaning harder on his cane than he had in a while, every part of him aching. His role in Tim's surgery had taken two hours.

Two exhilarating and challenging hours. He'd removed Tim's spleen, repaired a lacerated liver and located a perforation in his bowel, courtesy of a shard of bone from his fractured pelvis. Now the orthopods were doing their share of the job, pinning and plating the fractures.

'Ryan Harrison.' An older gentleman in a grey suit walked up to him in the corridor, his hand outstretched in greeting.

'Professor Blaketon.' Ryan couldn't hide his surprise at seeing his mentor from many years ago. 'You're a long way from Melbourne, sir. What brings you up to this part of the world?'

'I'm spending a month here as a visiting professor, a bit of north and south exchange.' The older man smiled. 'It was both a surprise and pleasure to watch you through the teaching glass and see you operating on that young motorcyclist.'

Warmth glowed inside him. 'It was touch and go for a bit—he'd lost a lot of blood.'

'But you pulled him through. Excellent job. A real treat for our visiting med students to be able to observe such a skilled clinician operate. There were no spare seats in the observation area.'

Ryan's heart sang. A professor of surgery, his mentor, had just praised his skills. 'Thank you, sir, that means a lot.'

'Hmm.' The older man took in the cane and then stared straight at him. 'Heard on the grapevine St Stephen's had let you go.'

'Yes. Six months ago.' What else could he say? That was the reality

'Damn fools.' The professor pulled out his wallet and plucked out a business card. 'You belong in Melbourne, Ryan, at the cutting edge. It's time to go back. If St Stephen's doesn't want you, Melbourne Metropolitan does. Ring Paul Dobson and set up an interview. I expect to see you in Theatre, part of the trauma team, when I get back there at the end of next week.'

Ryan took the proffered card, his mind racing. Melbourne. Home.

He twirled his cane. Operating in a major hospital again. Living in his beloved house again. Excitement bubbled through him. He couldn't believe it. At last, after all this time, he was finally getting his life back.

Everything he wanted and more. His wilderness experience had finished.

He shook the professor's hand firmly, words seeming inadequate to express how he really felt. 'Yes, sir. I'll see you then.'

The quietness of a Yakkaburra weeknight flowed around Sarah. Sam was fast asleep, clutching his first-place medal. The kitchen had been put to bed and a platter of cold chicken and avocado salad she'd prepared earlier sat waiting in the fridge next to a mango coulis. Ryan loved mango with ice cream.

She yawned and replayed a scene on the DVD. She expected Ryan to be back in Yakkaburra at around midnight, tired and hungry. She glanced at the clock. Not long now.

So much had happened that afternoon that the swimming carnival seemed days ago rather than hours. Between Jack and the Red Cross, she'd organised transport for the Nguyens to Cairns, finished her clinic and cooked a celebratory dinner for Sam.

Sam had been unusually quiet over his meal. He'd said he understood why Ryan couldn't be there but Sarah had caught the look of disappointment that had crossed his face before he'd hugged Drover.

A pain had cramped around her heart at the look. Every mother wanted to minimise her child's disappointment. Sam experienced more than his fair share.

Fatigue pressed in on her but she was determined to stay awake. Ryan had rung from the hire car as he'd been leaving Cairns and had almost immediately gone out of range. But during the truncated call she'd caught his excitement that Tim had miraculously pulled through. The sketchy details taunted her and she could hardly wait to hear the full story.

Car wheels crunched on the gravel and she ran to the front door, excitement humming along her veins.

Her porch light threw a yellow glow along the path. Ryan hauled himself out of the car and toward the house, looking pale with fatigue. Except for his eyes. They glowed with a brightness she'd not seen before.

She smiled up at him, marvelling at the deep thrill she got every time she saw him. 'Big day.'

He pulled her close. 'Huge.' He looked down into her eyes, his face animated despite the lines of exhaustion.

'I've got food.' She slung her arm around his waist and turned toward the house.

'Great, but I'd kill for a cup of tea.' He grinned and walked with her to the kitchen, sliding into the chair, hanging his cane off the back.

Sarah quickly placed the chicken and salad on the table and set the kettle to boil, feeling Ryan's gaze on her, loving the fact he enjoyed looking at her.

'How did Sam go in his other race?' Ryan piled his plate with food.

'He came fourth. He's gone to bed holding his medal but I'm sure he'll be over tomorrow afternoon to show you.' Sarah carried the teapot and mugs over to the table and sat down. 'So how's Tim?'

'Intubated, in Intensive Care and on observation for fat embolism and disseminated intravascular coagulation. The next couple of days will be pretty telling.'

'But at least he's got this far.' She sipped her tea. 'So, did Phillip Leighton operate?'

'No. He was caught up with a complicated bowel resection.' Ryan's face broke into a huge smile. 'I was given visiting surgeon status and I operated on Tim.'

Excitement and surprise cascaded through her. 'Oh, Ryan, that is so fantastic.'

He reached out across the table and took her hand, caressing her palm with his thumb. 'It was like my accident had never happened and I was back in Melbourne doing multi-trauma surgery. Even my leg held up.' He gave a wry smile. 'Just. It was like finding the last piece of a jig-saw.'

His elation flowed into her. She blinked a couple of times as tears of happiness threatened to spill. Her tortured surgeon had come full circle. Walking around to him, she sat on his lap, hugging him tight. 'I always believed you could do it.'

He stroked her face, his expression heartfelt. 'I know. Thank you.' He dropped a kiss on her forehead. 'But it gets better.'

She leaned back to look at him. 'How?'

His voice trembled with exhilaration. 'I've been offered a job.'

'At Cairns Base?' Her heart sang and her mind raced. That was the perfect solution for them both. Sure there was some commuting involved but...

His eyes danced, his body quivered. 'On the trauma surgical team at Melbourne Metropolitan.'

Blood plunged to her feet, leaving her dizzy and light-headed. Her brain recoiled, trying to grasp his words yet rejecting them at the same time.

Ryan just grinned at her, absorbed in his own news.

Melbourne. 'I don't understand. You operated in Cairns but you have a job in Melbourne?'

He nodded. 'Talk about fate. Professor Blaketon, my mentor from medical school, is on sabbatical in Cairns. He and his group of medical students observed me from the teaching theatre and afterwards he offered me the job.'

He hugged her hard. 'Isn't that the most amazing and perfect thing? Oh, Sarah, it means going home.'

Going home. Leaving Yakkaburra. Her heart contracted in pain. Deep inside she'd known he'd leave one day but she'd kidded herself it might not happen.

She wanted to be happy for him but every fibre of her being cried out at her own loss. She forced out the words against a constricted throat, hoping they could sound happy. 'It's what you've worked for. When do you leave?' The words sounded hollow.

'Tomorrow. I start in seven days.'

Her stomach rolled as acid surged into it, rising to scald the back of her throat. She swallowed against the thick feeling. 'That's so quick.'

'I know. Who would believe that my accident led me to a better job then I had at St Stephen's?' He tucked her hair behind her ear. 'Come with me. You and Sam.'

His question stunned her with a pure happiness that equally confused her. She hadn't expected this. Yet she wanted it, desperately.

So many thoughts pounded at her she couldn't sort them to think clearly. 'Come to Melbourne with you?'

'Yes, it will be brilliant.' He couldn't stop smiling. 'My townhouse won awards for its design. Just think, no more cockroaches scuttling along floorboards, no more temperamental hot-water service or garden that verges on jungle. Instead, there's an ocean of hot water and a spa, a state-of-the-art heating and cooling system, the world's most amazingly comfortable lounge chairs, my library and my telescope…'

A chill seeped into her despite the humid heat. He'd loved renovating the Queenslander, bringing it part way back to its former glory. How could he so easily dismiss it? 'Don't forget your hi-fi system.'

He laughed, missing the sarcasm in her voice. 'And my home theatre system. I've missed it all so much.'

The chill inside her turned silver, glinting like sharp metal. Shades of life with David whispered inside her, getting louder by the moment. A lifestyle that came ahead of people. She slid off his lap, wrapping her arms around herself to stop the shaking.

He stood up and walked over to her. 'I know it's all come out of left field and is a lot to take in, but it'll be great. You'll love the townhouse.' He ran his hand through her hair.

She struggled to think against the wondrous feelings his touch always sparked.

'And you have a garden for Drover?'

For a moment he looked nonplussed. 'Ah, no, just a courtyard.'

'What about a place for Sam to shoot baskets and ride his bike?'

He shook his head. 'But there's a park not far away.'

The last few weeks flashed past her—the two of them working together as colleagues, all three of them laughing around the dinner table, Sam and Ryan working together on the house, the family-type picnics… Balancing work and family.

She broke away from him again. 'And while you're

working sixteen hours a day in the trauma team, what are Sam and I supposed to do?'

He tilted his head, slightly baffled. 'Sam will have a huge room, wireless broadband for his computer, and it's close to Barton College, and in a couple of years he'll be old enough to catch the tram to school. You can pick up a job as a GP if you want or just spend time with Sam. Money won't be an issue.'

She bit her lip as his words lanced her. He had it all planned out. He thought it so perfect, yet it was all so wrong. David had tried to plan her life without consultation and what a disaster that had turned out to be. She was never going down that road again.

He ran his hand along his neck, confusion on his face. 'The view of the bay is amazing, the kitchen is perfect—you'll just love it.'

Everything in her recoiled at the idea. 'Oh, yes, I'll just love a kitchen with no oven.' It was David all over again. Possessions. Prestige. Soulless accoutrements of life.

'I'll install a damn oven.' His smile faded. 'I thought you'd be happy for me, for us.'

The pain squeezed her heart so tight she didn't know if she could survive this. He couldn't see. He'd missed the point entirely that life would change so drastically it would drive them apart. 'Ryan, this is your dream job and dream life, it's not mine.'

'It could be our dream if you let it. Isn't it time you moved on with your life and took a risk?'

His words pummelled her and she wanted to put her hands over her ears and make them stop. Was she wrong? Was she throwing away happiness? She buried the sprout of doubt that rose inside her. She had to protect herself and Sam. 'Maybe David taught me a valuable lesson. All you've mentioned since you got here is going home to possessions. Sam and I are not possessions to be added to the ones you have.'

He started. 'Don't be ridiculous—of course you're not a possession. I have the utmost respect for you.'

Respect. Her heart bled at all the word did not say.

She knew now, with unwavering clarity, what she had to do. She dragged in a long breath, delaying for a moment the words she had to say. Words that would change her life and leave her grieving and alone. 'I have a job here, a life in Yakkaburra, Ryan. Sam and I can't follow you, tagging along on the edge of your life. I'm sorry, but I'm done trying to be part of someone else's dream when it's so far removed from my own.'

The bubble of happiness that had encapsulated him since his conversation with Professor Blaketon burst, the remnants choking him like a caul. All the way back to Yakkaburra he'd been planning their life together in Melbourne.

Never in his wildest dreams had he imagined she'd reject him.

Anger coiled in his belly like a snake ready to strike. 'You knew how much I missed Melbourne, that my ultimate goal was to return. Now you're begrudging the fact I want my old life back?'

She sighed. 'No, of course not. I just don't think your old life made you very happy.'

The fury surged. 'Really. So now you're an expert on me, are you?'

Resolve lined her pale face. 'No, but you're rushing back to a job and a house. What about the people in your life? Yakkaburra values you. When did anyone in Melbourne make contact with you in all the time you were here?'

Her incisive words cut into him but he pushed them away. He'd never needed anyone and he wasn't about to start now. 'Of course no one contacted me. I was hardly going to announce I was coming back here, to the back of nowhere.'

A shudder ran through her. 'No matter how much you want to hate this town, Yakkaburra took you in and healed you. It gave you people who cared, people who love you. It's people who matter, Ryan, not possessions. You're the local boy made good. You don't have to prove anything to anyone any more.'

People who love you. A glimmer of hope tried to take hold but the pain of her rejection doused it. Surely if she loved him, she'd come with him? 'I'm not proving anything to anyone. Hell, I'm getting my life back. I can't live here, Sarah, you must know that.'

She jutted her chin and sighed. 'I'm not asking you to stay. I always knew you would leave. I'm just asking you if this will really make you happy.'

His brain shuddered at her complete lack of understanding. 'Of course it will make me happy. It's everything I've ever wanted. I've worked too hard to walk away from this job. I deserve it.'

She stared at him, her eyes luminous with a myriad of emotions, but her pain shone the brightest.

This was insane. He threw his hands out in front of him. 'Will you at least come and visit me or I can come and visit you and Sam once I've settled into the job?'

She bit her lip. 'How would that change anything?'

Desperation clawed at him. 'Please, Sarah, come with me. Why are you throwing away our chance at happiness?'

'If you can't understand then we have no chance.' Her words stung, their rejection harsh.

She tossed her head in that familiar decisive action and walked to the front door, pulling it open. 'Goodbye, Ryan. I hope your job and your house give you the fulfilment you believe they will.'

He hesitated. This wasn't how it was supposed to be, ending with her rejection of everything he held dear. Not raw, jagged and bleeding, with a hurt that made his leg pain feel like a tickle.

Every part of him roared in protest. He didn't want to leave her. He knew her pain was equal to his.

But he wasn't going to beg.

'I'll speak to Sam before I go.' He walked out, staring straight ahead. It was time to restart his life.

CHAPTER TEN

SARAH kicked off her shoes at the door, dumped her bag in the entrance and walked into the house, welcoming the cool breeze of the air-conditioner against her hot and sticky skin.

'Hi, Dr Rigby.'

'Hello, Abbey, how are things?' Sarah mustered a smile of greeting for the babysitter.

The seventeen-year-old pulled the white earbud head-phones out of her ears and frowned. 'Sam didn't want to do much today. I tried to get him to shoot baskets, but he just ate his afternoon tea and watched some TV. Now he's out on the back steps, sitting with Drover.' She picked up her bag. 'I hope he's not getting sick.'

Sarah's heart flinched. 'I'll go and talk to him. Thanks for helping out, Abbey.'

'No probs. Any time.' She put her earphones back in, humming as she closed the front door behind her.

Sarah took in a deep breath, walked through the kitchen and stood looking out through the fly-wire door. Sam sat with his back up against the house, staring out toward the old Queenslander, Drover by his side. He had something on his lap but she couldn't quite make it out.

Dealing with her grief was one thing. Keeping it together and helping Sam work through his was another thing altogether. Her piercing hurt twisted at the loss marked so clearly on his face.

He misses Ryan so much.

So do I.

The ever-present haunting question repeated itself like a soundtrack on a loop. Should she have accepted Ryan's offer? She pushed the unsettling words away. Instant gratification didn't bring happiness. Without compromise, she and Ryan had no future. But how could you compromise when offered a *fait accompli*?

Grabbing two plastic cups and a jug of cordial, she stepped outside and sat down next to Sam. She ruffled his hair. 'Hey, mate.'

Sam sniffed. 'Hi, Mum.' He snuggled in next to her, still her little boy when times were tough.

'What have you got there?' She looked at the khaki fabric that lay across his lap, damp in places.

Sam immediately pushed it over to his left side, away from her. 'Nothing.'

A flash of metal glinted in the sunshine. *Ryan's overalls.* The ones he'd always worn when he'd been working on the house. She closed her eyes and forced back the tears that threatened to spill. Sam was holding onto a tangible part of a precious memory, their times together at the house. 'Where did you get Ryan's overalls from?'

Sam hesitated for a moment before the words rushed out. 'The rubbish skip. Mr Taggerty put up a FOR SALE sign today and then Tom came over and dumped a heap of stuff in the skip.' Defiance streaked his face. 'I asked first before I took them.'

She squeezed his shoulders, desperately trying to stay on top of things. 'Good boy.'

She could hardly believe that in less than a week Ryan had set in motion a process that virtually removed all traces of his three months in Yakkaburra. It was like his time here had been a blip on the radar of his life, an unplanned detour. Nothing more.

'Why did he have to go?' Sam clutched the overalls with one hand and Sarah with the other.

The same question had been going round and round in her head for three days. 'He told you why, Sam. He came here to get well and he did that. Now he's back in Melbourne, doing the job he loves.'

'But he liked it here, he said so.'

The concrete logic of an eight-year-old hit her hard. 'I know, but it was a bit like a long holiday for him and now the holiday's finished. He likes Melbourne more.'

'That sucks.'

She sighed. 'Yeah it does.' Making a big effort to stay positive, she forced a smile. 'We've got something to look forward to, though. Someone nice will buy the house and finish renovating it. Maybe a family—that would be great, wouldn't it? You'd have some playmates.'

'S'pose.' He took a long draught from his drink.

'Want to have a swim at the pool before dinner?' Distraction technique might just work. Heaven knew, in desperation she was using it herself.

'Can we go on the water slide?' A spark of interest filled his eyes.

'Sure. Why not?' At least she could scream coming down the slide and no one would notice.

'OK.' Sam stood up and walked inside, carrying the overalls, his gait more subdued than usual.

Drover put his head on her lap, doleful brown eyes staring straight at her.

She stroked his ears. 'I knew he'd leave, so it shouldn't hurt this much, Drover. But it does. It hurts more than anything I've ever known.'

Ryan stepped back from the telescope. The *Spirit of Tasmania* chugged her way down the bay, her red hull slicing through the gentle waves of a warm summer evening. He checked his messages. Nothing.

He snapped his phone shut and pulled on a light jacket. His body thermostat hadn't caught up with coming south, and after the heat of far north Queensland he was constantly cold, despite it being a Melbourne summer.

Tonight was the first quiet night he'd had since returning, and he planned to enjoy it. Home had always been a delicious haven from work. Anticipating this time had kept him going. The last weeks had been frantic. Jam-packed with settling back into the house, settling into the job. Settling.

Except he was anything but settled.

Flicking on the stereo, he set it to random selection, anticipating the soothing sounds of his favourite music. He walked toward the kitchen, catching sight of the current book he'd started reading. The one he'd picked up ten times and put down again.

Work kept him focused—his operating schedule, tutorials with medical students, department meetings, none of it gave him time to think about anything other than the job. But away from work his mind wandered.

Always back to Yakkaburra.

To Sarah. And Sam.

They'd spent so much time together. He really missed Sam's enthusiastic approach to life, his thirst to learn, the way his large emerald eyes looked up at him, a combination of trust and awe. *Except for the sorrow you put into his eyes when you told him you were leaving.*

Raw anger jetted up inside him. He still couldn't believe Sarah hadn't come with him, that she was denying all three of them happiness. How could she question his choice in coming back here and reclaiming his life? She should look to herself and do something about her own life, move on from her marriage.

His heart started to pound in agitation. He was back where he belonged. He'd worked damn hard for this life. As if a surgeon could stay in Yakkaburra with antiquated equipment.

It didn't bother you when you applied for funding.

That voice kept popping into his head at unexpected moments. Damn it, he wasn't going to think about Yakkaburra. Or Sarah. It was over. Finished. History.

He pulled open the fridge, his growling stomach craving food.

A stick of celery, a bag of carrots, half a red pepper, butter, milk and some eggs stared back at him.

He could make an omelette. His stomach immediately rejected the idea.

Chocolate cake.

He grabbed the eggs, milk and butter, dumping them on the bench. He'd make his grandmother's cake. A small thrill of achievement whizzed through him. He'd got pretty good at making that cake in Yakkaburra.

There's no oven in this kitchen.

Frustration, laced with an inexplicable sense of loss, sent him back to the lounge room. He didn't need cake anyway. He sat down in his favourite soft leather chair that hugged him close and picked up his book, concentrating hard on the words.

He reread the same paragraph three times.

The music distracted him. He turned it off.

The silence taunted him.

His fingers itched to do something, create something, to feel the texture of wood beneath them again. He tossed the book aside and ran his hands through his hair, a foreign sense of desolation crawling through him. His house had always been his oasis, his pride and joy.

But Yakkaburra, Sarah and Sam clung to him like a second skin, no matter how hard he tried to ignore them.

Sam's laughter played across his mind. *Hey, Ryan, can you show me how to use that jig-saw?* Sarah's smile hovered, a constant image so vivid in his memory that he could almost reach out and touch it.

You're rushing back to a job and a house. What about the people in your life? Sarah's concerned expression tore at him.

He'd never needed people. As a kid he'd learned to do without them, yet now he hated his message service for the lack of personal texts. He sat forward, an idea popping into his head. He'd throw a party, get back into the social part of his life. He grabbed a notepad. Who could he invite?

A flood of names poured out of his head, scorching

him. His stomach turned over and he gagged. Every single name belonged to a person in Yakkaburra. He lived in Melbourne but he had no connections there, apart from the hospital.

He tossed the notepad to the floor and stood up, pacing across his thick, plush, sound-absorbing carpet—even his restlessness denied a voice.

Everything that had given him pleasure before his accident now mocked him with its soullessness.

It's people who matter, Ryan, not possessions.

He gripped his cane, realisation crushing him with its hurtful truth. He'd just walked away from the best thing that had ever happened to him to come back to this. None of his state-of-the-art things mattered.

And his job?

He slumped into a dining chair.

Of course Sarah hadn't come to Melbourne with him. He'd wanted to plug her and Sam into his life without making a single change. He'd tried to organise her, just like David had, with no regard for what she wanted in her life.

He groaned. That wasn't love.

Love.

His breath whooshed out of his lungs, his chest muscles screaming.

Oh, God, he loved her. Why had it taken this long for him to realise?

He'd been so fixed on his own life, craving to have his pre-accident life back, that he'd missed the gem in the rubbish heap of his post-accident life.

I have the upmost respect for you. He cringed as the words he'd said boomed in his head at megaphone volume. He loved her but she didn't know. And he loved Sam.

What a fool he'd been.

He sat up straight in the chair. If his accident had taught him anything, it had taught him that you had to fight for what you wanted. He'd been fighting for the wrong things.

So this time he'd get it right.

He stood up and walked into his office. Bringing up an Internet browser, he typed in, 'Queensland Department of Health'.

Sarah's chest burned as she drove past the old Queenslander, catching sight of the bright red SOLD sign pasted onto the real estate agent's board. 'That's it then. His final connection with Yakkaburra's been severed.' She spoke the words out loud, needing to hear them to reinforce their full meaning. 'You can't hold out any false hope now.'

For over a month she'd let her imagination occasionally wander, daydreaming that if the house didn't sell Ryan might come back. She knew it was fatuous but on lonely nights it kept her going.

But real life started today. She put her car into gear and drove to work for her afternoon clinic.

'Hi, boss.' Jenny smiled, her tone gently teasing. Everyone in town had been gentle with her these last few weeks, which she appreciated. But it was time to get back to normal. 'Anything vital?' She accepted the proffered mail.

'There's some department memos about the medical circuit specialists and Tim's referral notes. He's in rehab but looking to be discharged soon.'

'That's excellent news.' She turned to go.

'One more thing.' Jenny hesitated and then started speaking quickly. 'You've got a late meeting with a couple of department officials about the funding for the laparoscope for Theatre.'

Ryan's project. She swallowed against the lump in her throat. 'You should cancel it. We no longer have a surgeon.'

She looked contrite. 'I tried but the bureaucrat on the end of the line said—she put on a mock, officious voice—"A circuit surgeon will be in attendance and it is imperative the GP attend." A streak of hope lit up in the nurse's eyes. 'Perhaps they've decided to use Yakkaburra as a surgical centre.'

'Well, I'll be needing another doctor, then.' A surge of anger sparked at the bureaucracy and faded just as quickly. It would be great for the town. Sarah shrugged. 'I guess I have to go to the meeting, then.' She hiked her bag higher up her shoulder. 'Give me five minutes to familiarise myself with the funding document so I don't look like a fool in the meeting, and then buzz me for the first patient.'

'You got it.' Jenny swivelled back to the computer.

Sarah adjusted the air-conditioning, stowed her handbag in a cupboard and put the mail on her desk. She opened the bright blue folder and turned to the first page.

Her pager vibrated against her belt as Jenny's running feet sounded in the corridor.

Jenny's face, white with shock, appeared in the doorway. 'A balcony's collapsed at one of the old derelict houses by the river. A group of kids have gone down with it.'

Fractures. Crush injuries. Her mind raced, running

through what they'd need. She grabbed Jenny's arm and rushed toward the treatment room. Tossing bags at the nurse, she started loading intravenous kits and dressings into them. 'Do we know how many people have been hurt?'

'Jack doesn't know for sure but the school's reported twenty-five students absent.'

Sarah closed her eyes for a moment, catching her breath. 'I'm activating the community emergency plan.' She jammed a hard hat on Jenny's head as well as her own and then struggled into her emergency overalls. 'Jack will have rung rural ambulance and the state emergency service but you need to come with me because even with the paramedics we're going to need as many hands as we can.'

As she reversed the car out of the clinic car park she spoke on her hands-free phone. 'Jack, I'm five minutes away. Get Cairns Base and Innisfail on radio and put the chopper on standby.'

'Will do, Doc.'

She navigated the car through four tight turns and found the house.

Chaos greeted her.

Splintered wood, twisted metal and blood. Screaming girls, sobbing boys and silent, white-faced teenagers wandering in circles.

Her gut clenched at the sight. 'Jenny, get blankets around the walking wounded and triage them. Any cuts and bruises, deal with them. Slings on fractured arms, you know the drill.' She ran toward the area that once been weeds growing below a veranda.

'Sarah, over here.' Jack heaved at a beam.

Sarah picked her way over, her heart in her mouth at what Jack had found. She saw a girl buried under the rubble. 'We're going to get you out, sweetie, hang on.'

Sirens screamed, getting louder, meaning help was closer.

'On my count.' She nodded at Jack as they both gripped the beam. 'One, two three.' Somehow she managed to move it sideways. Dropping to her knees, she spoke to the girl. 'What's your name?'

'Ellen.' The word came out on a sob.

'I'm Sarah and...' A shadow fell across her and she looked up.

A tall, dark-haired man in medical-emergency overalls squatted down next to Ellen, his expression caring and concerned. 'And I'm Ryan. We're both doctors and we're going to help you.'

Ryan. Shock immobilised her for the briefest second. But she had no time to wonder why he was there—she was just thankful these kids had another doctor to treat them. Nothing existed beyond this emergency. No matter how she felt about him, no matter the pain and grief he'd caused, she needed medical back-up. She'd take what she could get.

'You take Ellen, I'll keep on doing triage.' She pushed herself up, ignoring the flash of longing in his eyes, instead remembering his grim expression and curt nod.

She assessed ten more patients, inserted IVs and prioritised the dispatch to hospital. Broken bones and sprains were the most common injury and she gave thanks they'd got off so lightly.

Occasionally she found herself scanning the site for Ryan. Each time he was head down, working with a patient. Once she saw him stretch and rub his leg. She bit her lip at the wave of emotion that swamped her at the familiar action.

'Sarah! Over here.' Jack's frantic voice called her.

She picked her way carefully over the debris. 'What's up?'

A teenage boy lay still, a metal veranda pole driven through his leg.

She reached for his carotid pulse. Thready. Weak.

'Ryan.' She called out his name, loud and clear, as she unravelled the IV tube and primed it.

Instantly he was beside her. The edge of her anxiety for this boy dulled, knowing Ryan was there. She heard his half-swallowed expletive when he saw the pole.

'Jack, find out from one of the walking wounded what this kid's name is.' Ryan crouched down next to the patient.

The boy's eyes fluttered open and closed.

'He needs two lines.' He half turned, waved his arm and called for the paramedics. 'Bring the portable monitor—now.' He turned back to the patient and gently pressed his shoulder, trying to rouse him.

'Get a reading.' The instruction came out unusually brusque.

She understood his concern completely. Wrapping the BP cuff around the boy's arm, she quickly pumped up the pressure. 'Seventy-five on forty.'

'He's bleeding into his leg.' He attached the ECG dots to the lad's chest. 'Let's hope it missed the femoral artery.'

Sarah hoped so, too. She pulled the tourniquet tight and tried to locate a vein for the drip. Her fingers probed as she willed a vein to bulge up. Nothing.

'Is Mitchell going to be all right?' A scared voice came behind them.

'We're doing everything we can. You head back to Nurse Jenny, OK?' Ryan spoke softly but firmly.

'He's in venous shutdown.' Sarah clicked the plastic release button. 'I'll try the other arm.'

'We don't need this thing moving and doing even more damage.' Ryan packed dressings around the entry site, stabilising the pole. 'Are you in? He needs fluid.' His voice sounded agitated.

He had every right to sound that way. Mitchell's life hung in the balance. A small vein rose against her fingers. She carefully slid the cannula through the skin and into place, knowing this was her only chance.

Holding her breath, she prayed that she wouldn't accidentally go through the vein.

She pulled out the trocar. Blood came back. 'I'm in.'

'Well done.'

Ryan's whispered words caressed her. *No, don't go there. He's a team player, he always gives praise where it's due.*

'What about his leg?' She looked into his serious face, his cheeks drawn with worry.

The ECG monitor beeped as the boy's pulse rate dropped.

Ryan grabbed the tourniquet, frantically searching for another vein. 'He won't make it to Cairns. Pray we can keep up the circulating volume until we get him into Theatre at Yakkaburra. I don't fancy doing an amputation right here, do you?'

Adrenaline surged into her at the thought. 'Let's move him out, then.'

Ryan nodded as he inserted the second line.

'Mike, bring the stretcher, we need to move him to Yakkaburra now! Jenny, ring Karen and tell her we're on our way to Theatre.'

The ride to the hospital took five minutes but felt like fifty. With amazing speed they managed to transfer Mitchell into Theatre.

Sarah couldn't remember ever administering an anaesthetic so quickly. As she went through each step her ears strained to hear every single beep of the monitor, willing it to stay stable. If he arrested before Ryan could tie off the bleeding vessels, it would be really hard to bring him back.

Telling his mother her son had died would be even harder.

'Sarah?' Ryan's eyes met hers. 'Ready?'

'Ready.' She dropped her gaze from his. Working with him was tough enough without remembering how those eyes had sparkled when they'd made love.

The moment this surgery was over, and Mitchell was safely on the air ambulance to Cairns, she never had to see Ryan again. If she kept reminding herself of that she'd get through.

Ryan worked slowly, gaining control of each blood vessel, artery and vein before he removed the pole. Setting up the field to minimise the chance of a massive bleed when the pole came out.

'I'm removing the pole.' The words came out low, understating the full significance of the event.

Sarah clenched her fists, her eyes and ears glued to the monitors. Would Mitchell's barely maintained fluid load cope? She prayed Ryan's natural diligence in rechecking every ligature would stand him in good stead.

Slowly, millimetre by millimetre, the pole rose in Ryan's gloved hand.

'I'm out.' Ryan dropped the pole into the rubbish bin. 'Checking for oozing. How's he holding up, Sarah?'

She blew out a breath. 'Tachycardic but stable. How's his pedal pulse?' His leg needed good blood flow to survive this injury.

'Not too bad, considering. He's going to have one hell of a scar.' He raised his brows. 'I might have just found someone to compete with.'

She smiled despite all her intentions to stay immune to him. The high soared through her then plummeted down again. *Except you won't be here to compare.* Regret poured through her. She had to keep her guard up or she wouldn't get through this. 'Morphine, ten milligrams.' She announced the administration of the drug, refocusing on being Ryan's colleague and nothing more.

'Antibiotic lavage, Karen,' the surgeon instructed.

The stage had been set. Just two professionals thrown together by fate and working side by side for one last time.

The pain around her heart crushed her with its ferocity.

'Sarah.' Ryan's melodic voice rolled across her, calling her from behind.

She paused on her walk down the corridor and squared her shoulders. Mitchell had been evacuated. Three children were in hospital for observation and for plaster checks, and Ellen had gone by road ambulance to Cairns. All in all they'd treated thirty teenagers and a few overwrought parents.

But after *this* emergency she didn't want to debrief with Ryan. She wanted to be as far away from him as possible. She didn't care if that would leave her with un-answered questions about his sudden reappearance. The sale of the house had probably brought him back. He'd sign the papers for the house and leave again.

The sooner he left town, the better.

She turned and looked straight at him, forcing her professional mask onto her face. 'Yes?' The word snapped out.

He flinched. 'Can I come and see you at home so we can talk?'

She folded her arms across her chest to keep her heart from jumping right out of her chest. 'No. I don't want Sam to see you. He doesn't deserve any more pain.'

The flash of pain in his own eyes almost undid her resolve.

'What about now?'

'I'm too busy now.' She tossed her head. 'I'm really late for a meeting with the department and I've already kept the bureaucrats and the circuit surgeon waiting.'

A smile tugged at his lips. 'I doubt they'll mind.'

His mild tone infuriated her. 'Really? Well, how things function in Yakkaburra is no longer your concern.' She turned to go.

'Actually, it is.'

She froze at his words. White noise roared in her ears and her head spun. His house had been sold. His job was in Melbourne. He'd completely cut his ties with Yakkaburra. None of this made sense. 'What do you mean?'

'Can we talk about this somewhere private, rather than in the middle of the corridor?' He put his hands out in supplication.

As much as she wanted to, she couldn't deny him this reasonable request. She sighed. 'Let's go outside.' She pushed open a door that led to a courtyard ringed with tree ferns. A two-seater wooden seat nestled in the shade and a small fountain bubbled in the corner, the sound calming. Patients often came here but today it was mercifully empty.

Ryan sat down, stretching his leg out in front of him, tension running though his body like a coiled spring.

Sarah continued to stand, not trusting herself to sit next to him, inhaling his scent of soap and something undefineably male, feeling the heat of his body pouring into hers. *I can't do this.*

'Sarah, please, sit.' His voice implored and for the first time she really looked at him. Deep lines were carved into his cheeks, dark rings hovered under his eyes, which held some shadows. Shadows that hadn't been there when he'd left Yakkaburra.

She sat with her thigh wedged against the side of the seat, creating a sizeable gap between them. 'Why are you here?'

'Because I've been a bloody idiot.'

'You won't get an argument from me on that point.'

He gave her a wry smile. 'I left myself wide open for that one.'

She didn't want to do this, banter with him. She wanted this conversation over as soon as possible. 'Seriously, Ryan, why are you here?'

'I'm here for a lot of things, but first I'm here to apologise to you and to Sam.' He reached for her hand.

She tried to move it away from him, to avoid his touch completely, but she couldn't. She craved his touch too much. She hated herself for being so weak.

His warm, familiar fingers wrapped themselves around her hand, sending tendrils of aching longing through her.

She tried to steel her heart.

His contrite gaze caught hers. 'It was incredibly arrogant of me to expect you to up sticks and join me in my Melbourne life. I thought it would be the most perfect thing to have you and Sam, and my old life back. I realise now that it completely devalued your life here. I'm really sorry, Sarah.'

She heard the words but couldn't make sense of them. 'You came all the way up here to say sorry?'

'Yes… no… I mean…' He ran his hand across the back of his neck. 'Hell, I'm making a mess of this.' He took in a deep breath. 'The whole time I was in Yakkaburra I was so focused on what I'd lost and how to get it all back that I didn't see what I'd gained.'

A tiny spark of hope lit up inside her but she squashed it, focusing on being rational. That would protect her. 'What did you gain, Ryan?'

'I gained this town that cloaked me in caring, I gained a wonderful and fulfilling relationship with Sam and I gained you.' He squeezed her hand. 'I want to be with you.'

He'd wanted her and Sam to be with him before so what did this mean?

I want to be with you. Her knees started to shake, her heart pounded. Did he want to come back? Surely not. 'What about your job? Part of who you are is a surgeon and you can't have cutting-edge surgery here.'

He leaned foreword, his face earnest. 'My job is important to me but it's not as important as you. Call me slow, but it took going back to Melbourne to realise that. The job was great but there was nothing else in my life.'

He kissed her hand. 'I actually lost more by leaving Yakkaburra than I gained by returning to Melbourne. I want to be a surgeon but I want to be part of a family, too. Our family. I love you, Sarah.'

Her head spun with his words. He loved her. He wanted a family. She put her hand over his. 'I love you, too. I think a part of me has always loved you.'

He stroked her face. 'I'm glad I finally caught up, then.' Pulling her close, he wrapped his arm around her shoulders.

She snuggled in. 'It's a shame you sold the house.'

'I didn't sell it.' A ripple of happiness ran through the words.

She sat up straight and looked at him. 'But the sold sign…'

He grinned. 'It's a metaphor. I'd never valued that house, it was just left to me and I saw it as a noose around my neck. It took three months of working on it for me to realise how much it meant to me. Part of me is in the essence of that house.'

He pulled her back against his shoulder. 'The sticker is a commitment to the home it will become. Our home. That's if you want to live there.'

Her heart soared that he'd asked for her opinion. 'Of course I want to live there, as long as I have some say on the colour of the paint.' She laughed and caught sight of her watch and the time. Torn by professional duties and the desire to never leave Ryan's arms again. 'Ryan, I've got this meeting I have to take with the circuit surgeon.'

His eyes sparkled. 'You're having it.'

Realisation dawned. 'That's why you arrived today.'

She ran her hand along his chest, resting it over his heart. 'Thank goodness you did, on two fronts.'

He nodded and dropped a light kiss onto her head. 'The department boffins are relaxing at the pub—we'll do the meeting tomorrow. But I'm your regional circuit surgeon. It means some time in Cairns, some time in Innisfail, but with increased funding more time in Yakkaburra.'

She gazed straight at him, phrasing the question she had to ask. 'Are you sure about giving up the big city and big hospital life?'

'Absolutely.' His face glowed with his decision. 'There's nothing there for me. I've made my peace with Yakkaburra and I belong here. There are good people in this town but most importantly there's you.'

The thrill of being loved almost took her breath away and she blinked back tears of joy, unable to speak.

'You once said to me that it was people who count, not possessions. And you're right, although the first thing I'm going to do is install a decent a hot-water service.'

She laughed, revelling in the joy of being with the man she loved. The man who made her laugh, who made her feel so blessed and cherished.

He stretched his leg out further and pulled a small wooden box out of his pocket. The polished wood gleamed in the sunshine, displaying a myriad of colours in the wood. He placed it on the palm of his hand. 'I love working with wood so it seemed natural to make this for the woman I love.'

She gazed at it, knowing the amount of time that would have gone into creating it. 'It's beautiful. Thank you.'

'I made a larger one for Sam.' A slight hesitancy lingered on the words.

She stroked his arm, reassuring him that Sam would welcome him back with open arms. 'He'll love it, he'll keep his treasures in it.'

He held the box out toward her and gave her a wry smile. 'I'd get down on bended knee but it doesn't bend very well.' He flicked open the box and a dark blue Queensland sapphire sparkled next to two diamonds. 'Sarah, will you love me, marry me and join me in renovating?'

She gazed into his eyes brimming with love. 'Will you love me, marry me and join me in raising Sam?'

Hope moved across his face. 'And our other children?'

Sarah thought she'd burst with happiness. 'And our other children.'

'I will.'

'And so will I.'

She raised her lips to his, their kiss sealing their commitment and their love, paving the way for their future together.

1206 Gen Std HB

MILLS & BOON®
Live the emotion

JANUARY 2007 HARDBACK TITLES

ROMANCE™

Royally Bedded, Regally Wedded *Julia James*	0 263 19556 2
The Sheikh's English Bride *Sharon Kendrick*	0 263 19557 0
Sicilian Husband, Blackmailed Bride *Kate Walker*	0 263 19558 9
At the Greek Boss's Bidding *Jane Porter*	0 263 19559 7
The Spaniard's Marriage Demand *Maggie Cox*	0 263 19560 0
The Prince's Convenient Bride *Robyn Donald*	0 263 19561 9
One-Night Baby *Susan Stephens*	0 263 19562 7
The Rich Man's Reluctant Mistress *Margaret Mayo*	0 263 19563 5
Cattle Rancher, Convenient Wife *Margaret Way*	0 263 19564 3
Barefoot Bride *Jessica Hart*	0 263 19565 1
Their Very Special Gift *Jackie Braun*	0 263 19566 X
Her Parenthood Assignment *Fiona Harper*	0 263 19567 8
The Maid and the Millionaire *Myrna Mackenzie*	0 263 19568 6
The Prince and the Nanny *Cara Colter*	0 263 19569 4
A Doctor Worth Waiting For *Margaret McDonagh*	0 263 19570 8
Her L.A. Knight *Lynne Marshall*	0 263 19571 6

HISTORICAL ROMANCE™

Innocence and Impropriety *Diane Gaston*	0 263 19748 4
Rogue's Widow, Gentleman's Wife *Helen Dickson*	0 263 19749 2
High Seas to High Society *Sophia James*	0 263 19750 6

MEDICAL ROMANCE™

A Father Beyond Compare *Alison Roberts*	0 263 19784 0
An Unexpected Proposal *Amy Andrews*	0 263 19785 9
Sheikh Surgeon, Surprise Bride *Josie Metcalfe*	0 263 19786 7
The Surgeon's Chosen Wife *Fiona Lowe*	0 263 19787 5

MILLS & BOON®

Live the emotion

1206 Gen Std LP

JANUARY 2007 LARGE PRINT TITLES

ROMANCE™

Mistress Bought and Paid For *Lynne Graham*	0 263 19415 9
The Scorsolini Marriage Bargain *Lucy Monroe*	0 263 19416 7
Stay Through the Night *Anne Mather*	0 263 19417 5
Bride of Desire *Sara Craven*	0 263 19418 3
Married Under the Italian Sun *Lucy Gordon*	0 263 19419 1
The Rebel Prince *Raye Morgan*	0 263 19420 5
Accepting the Boss's Proposal *Natasha Oakley*	0 263 19421 3
The Sheikh's Guarded Heart *Liz Fielding*	0 263 19422 1

HISTORICAL ROMANCE™

The Bride's Seduction *Louise Allen*	0 263 19379 9
A Scandalous Situation *Patricia Frances Rowell*	0 263 19380 2
The Warlord's Mistress *Juliet Landon*	0 263 19381 0

MEDICAL ROMANCE™

The Midwife's Special Delivery *Carol Marinelli*	0 263 19331 4
A Baby of His Own *Jennifer Taylor*	0 263 19332 2
A Nurse Worth Waiting For *Gill Sanderson*	0 263 19333 0
The London Doctor *Joanna Neil*	0 263 19334 9
Emergency in Alaska *Dianne Drake*	0 263 19531 7
Pregnant on Arrival *Fiona Lowe*	0 263 19532 5

0107 Gen Std HB

MILLS & BOON®

Live the emotion

FEBRUARY 2007 HARDBACK TITLES

ROMANCE™

The Marriage Possession *Helen Bianchin*   978 0 263 19572 9
The Sheikh's Unwilling Wife *Sharon Kendrick* 978 0 263 19573 6
The Italian's Inexperienced Mistress *Lynne Graham*
                                                  978 0 263 19574 3
The Sicilian's Virgin Bride *Sarah Morgan*   978 0 263 19575 0
The Rich Man's Bride *Catherine George*   978 0 263 19576 7
Wife by Contract, Mistress by Demand *Carole Mortimer*
                                                  978 0 263 19577 4
Wife by Approval *Lee Wilkinson*   978 0 263 19578 1
The Sheikh's Ransomed Bride *Annie West*   978 0 263 19579 8
Raising the Rancher's Family *Patricia Thayer* 978 0 263 19580 4
Matrimony with His Majesty *Rebecca Winters*   978 0 263 19581 1
In the Heart of the Outback... *Barbara Hannay* 978 0 263 19582 8
Rescued: Mother-To-Be *Trish Wylie*   978 0 263 19583 5
The Sheikh's Reluctant Bride *Teresa Southwick*
                                                  978 0 263 19584 2
Marriage for Baby *Melissa McClone*   978 0 263 19585 9
City Doctor, Country Bride *Abigail Gordon*   978 0 263 19586 6
The Emergency Doctor's Daughter *Lucy Clark*   978 0 263 19587 3

HISTORICAL ROMANCE™

A Most Unconventional Courtship *Louise Allen* 978 0 263 19751 8
A Worthy Gentleman *Anne Herries*   978 0 263 19752 5
Sold and Seduced *Michelle Styles*   978 0 263 19753 2

MEDICAL ROMANCE™

His Very Own Wife and Child *Caroline Anderson*
                                                  978 0 263 19788 4
The Consultant's New-Found Family *Kate Hardy*
                                                  978 0 263 19789 1
A Child to Care For *Dianne Drake*   978 0 263 19790 7
His Pregnant Nurse *Laura Iding*   978 0 263 19791 4

MILLS & BOON®

0107 Gen Std LP

Live the emotion

FEBRUARY 2007 LARGE PRINT TITLES

ROMANCE™

Purchased by the Billionaire *Helen Bianchin*	978 0 263 19423 4
Master of Pleasure *Penny Jordan*	978 0 263 19424 1
The Sultan's Virgin Bride *Sarah Morgan*	978 0 263 19425 8
Wanted: Mistress and Mother *Carol Marinelli*	978 0 263 19426 5
Promise of a Family *Jessica Steele*	978 0 263 19427 2
Wanted: Outback Wife *Ally Blake*	978 0 263 19428 9
Business Arrangement Bride *Jessica Hart*	978 0 263 19429 6
Long-Lost Father *Melissa James*	978 0 263 19430 2

HISTORICAL ROMANCE™

Mistaken Mistress *Margaret McPhee*	978 0 263 19382 4
The Inconvenient Duchess *Christine Merrill*	978 0 263 19383 1
Falcon's Desire *Denise Lynn*	978 0 263 19384 8

MEDICAL ROMANCE™

The Sicilian Doctor's Proposal *Sarah Morgan*	978 0 263 19335 0
The Firefighter's Fiancé *Kate Hardy*	978 0 263 19336 7
Emergency Baby *Alison Roberts*	978 0 263 19337 4
In His Special Care *Lucy Clark*	978 0 263 19338 1
Bride at Bay Hospital *Meredith Webber*	978 0 263 19533 0
The Flight Doctor's Engagement *Laura Iding*	978 0 263 19534 7